The Traveler's League: Braxo's Escape

Written by Nick Goss
Cover Design: TS95 Studio
Illustrations: Tara Faul
Editor: SJS Editorial Service

Published by Nicholas Goss, Nashville, TN
Copyright © 2018 Nicholas Goss

Publisher's Note: This is a work of fiction. Names, characters, places, and incidents are a product of the author's imagination. Locales and public names are sometimes used for atmospheric purposes.
 Any resemblance to actual people, living or dead, or to business, companies, events, institutions, or locales is completely coincidental.

Printed in the United States of America
ISBN 978-1-7321815-3-3 (Paperback)

Note from the Author

Dear Reader,

I hope you enjoy reading this book as much as I enjoyed creating the story within it. The next story in this series is even better because of the feedback I receive from parents and children.

I highly value any feedback about my story, the writing, editing, artwork, etc. If you would please leave an honest review of this book, on the site from which you purchased it, it will help others make a more informed buying decision.

With all of my heart, thank you for purchasing this book! Now let's continue the adventure...

~ Nick

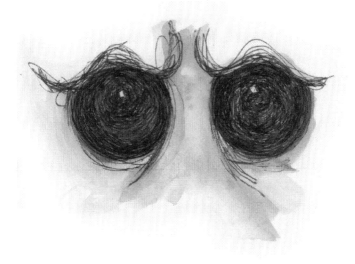

Braxo's Escape

The Traveler's League - Book 2

By Nick Goss

Table of Contents

*"You can only be brave
when you're scared."*

-The Traveler's Code, Article II.

Grumblebriar

    Lightning cracked through the smoky grey clouds overhead. The twisted branches of dead and dying redwood trees whistled as a thick, hot wind rolled through the forest. It was late afternoon but there were no sounds of roosting birds or small critters nesting. The 'whoosh' of the timepiece could barely be heard as Eva Mae appeared curled up in a ball, lying on her side. Luckily, there was no rain and the air was hot from the heat of an endless dry summer. She was soaked head to foot with salty ocean water.

"What's this?" a scratchy low voice boomed.

Eva Mae spun around to look, but nobody was behind her.

"Here. Look here, silly girl." The voice came from a large, wooden face in the trunk of an old gnarly tree.

"Did you just... talk?" Eva Mae gasped.

"Of course I talk! Who else do you see around here?" the tree grumbled.

Lightning streaked across the sky again, lower than before. The tree shuddered and moaned.

"That one was too close," the old tree complained. "My time's coming soon. Humph. Burned up like all the rest. Forest isn't like it used to be."

Eva Mae wasn't worried about lightning or concerned about the weather. Any chance she had to enjoy the outdoors was a special time for her. But she never thought for a moment that she would see something as extraordinary as a talking tree! The timepiece had taken her through four different worlds already and she had encountered strange creatures and dazzling places. The first world she traveled to was an island jungle full of wonderful animals and exciting vistas of waterfalls, sandy beaches, and double moonlit skies. The second world was the dimension that exists inside the mirrors of our world. Who knew that was a real place! It had been the perfect hiding spot from her mean foster parents who had thrown in the towel and decided to take her back to the orphanage only yesterday. A shadowy desert cave was all the third world seemingly had to offer, except for the strange ancient pictures scribbled on the walls, telling stories of strange monsters and odd people. The underwater world, the fourth destination the timepiece had taken her to, had almost killed her— but it was her favorite. It was a weightless universe of sea life and dancing crystal-blue wonders. Now the timepiece had brought her to a strange forest, with a talking tree. This world seemed both beautiful and broken. From the landscape of the forest to the grumpy ramblings of the old twisted tree in front of her, she could tell it had once been a lush, vibrant, happy place. But something had happened, something sinister and mean. There was a melancholy force poisoning this once peaceful land. A sadness hung in the air as the old tree waited to finally die.

"Well, what did the forest used to be like?" she asked the tree.

"It used to be alive!" he bellowed. "And green from the Crystal Mountains, to the river beyond the snows. Sunshine and rain in perfect balance, in one continuous spring. Morning dew to drink every day on every leaf of every tree, and cool, misty fogs to shake off the heat of long, beating summer days. A choir of stars to sing to you and keep you company at night, and a vast orchestra of critters scampering up and down every trunk and branch to keep you company throughout the day."

"It sounds like it was a wonderful place. I wish I could have seen it when it was pretty. It's still kinda pretty though," Eva Mae offered. "I never knew that a face and a voice would make a tree more interesting and beautiful. You, sir, have certainly shown me that!"

For a moment, the old tree stopped its bemoaning of how great the world used to be. The encounter of a young girl with a brave heart, an ear to listen, and a very agreeable attitude, awakened the playful kindness the great forest trees had once been known for.

"What's your name, child?"

"I'm Eva Mae. Not 'Eva.' Eva Mae… What's your name?"

"My name? No one has cared to ask me that since Green Dewin planted me here. That was a long time ago. I think I may have forgotten my name. Perhaps you could give me one? I think I'd like a new one anyway. Might as well enjoy something new before I get lapped up by that cursed lightning."

Eva Mae thought for a few seconds and said, "I'll call you 'GrumbleBriar.'"

"GrumbleBriar… hmmm… yes. That's good! I love it! I am GrumbleBriar and very pleased to meet you." The old tree seemed mighty satisfied with the new name. Every time he said it, he sounded like he was bragging about it.

"So what brings you to GrumbleBriar's forest, little one? You appeared rather suddenly. I was taking a nap, waiting for the lightning to finish me off, when I heard a strange whooshing sound. When I opened my eyes, there you were, curled up on the ground above my roots."

Eva Mae held out the timepiece and said, "This magic watch brought me here. It takes me to a different world every time I set it to a different hour."

"Oh? Is that so? Very interesting. Well, what time is it now?" GrumbleBriar asked.

"This is the 'five o'clock' world." Eve Mae held the watch close to his face.

"The five o'clock world, eh? I've never heard Sirihbaz called that before."

Sirihbaz. A perfectly odd name for a perfectly odd place.

The old tree continued, "It's been ages since a girl has been chosen to travel. A girl once set this entire world on its path to destruction. Perhaps things have come full circle now. Interesting, indeed."

Eva Mae didn't talk. She just listened. GrumbleBriar told her the tale of Sarah Grankel. How she arrived with the timepiece and had brought a friend with her, a young boy named Bradford. While they were exploring the Crystal Mountains, he slipped and fell into a ravine. Sarah couldn't reach him and told him she would get help. She used the timepiece and vanished to another world, but never came back.

"I think she meant to come back, but I suspect the timepiece didn't let her, or perhaps she lost it. Who knows. But it was no matter. Bradford was left behind here in Sirihbaz."

"What happened to him?" Eva Mae asked.

"He grew hateful and was greatly embittered. The WolliPog took him in, but as he grew up, he became a dark and mean soul. Unfortunately, he uncovered the magic secrets of Sirihbaz and became an evil mage. He's been enslaving the WolliPog and seeking revenge on the travelers who pass through here ever since. His resentment and thirst for power and vengeance has brought this world to the sad state you see before you.

"You're in danger, Eva Mae. If he finds you, he'll kill you and take the timepiece. Who knows what terrors he could bring to other worlds if he escaped Sirihbaz? You must go. Leave Sirihbaz as soon as the timepiece will allow."

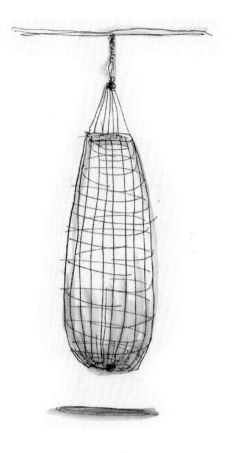

Field of Ruin

In the darkest part of the forest, a tangled mess of thorn bushes and thick brush kept most animals and people from seeing what was hidden. The trees grew so closely together, the trunks bumped into each other and twisted around each other, forming natural walls, rings, mazes, and dead ends. Many of the dead dry branches sprawled their brittle arms out in a way that blocked the sunlight and wove a ceiling of deadwood. The very thickest part of the forest, what used to be call the Green Heart, was now a nightmare of tangles and mazes, with no woodland creatures. Most creatures avoided the Green Heart altogether, and if passing by, went out of their way to avoid it. The trees and brush there were all dead, meaning they grew no leaves or moss. They were all rotted old trees that somehow kept growing into each other, without the need for rain or sun. They were dead but lived. Like the bare gray trees of a cold, snowless February that kept on growing without ever birthing new leaves. The Green Heart had become the cursed undead center of the forest that spread for a good mile in all directions.

Eva Mae could go no further. She had walked for hours and her legs ached from the hike. Her body was tired, and her stomach growled with hunger. But the worst part was that her feet were terribly sore. She had arrived in Sirihbaz wearing no shoes. She had only a pocketed dress that was still damp from her adventure in the underwater world. The sky darkened and night was on its way so when the tired little traveler ran into the wall of trees at the edge of the Green Heart, she gave up her adventures for the day and looked for shelter. All along the rotten wooden wall she searched. There were no openings or passes. No trees wide enough apart to allow her to squeeze between and get under the canopy of dead, tangled branches above.

But on the side of a wooded hill that ran along the western wall of the Green Heart, there was a large, flat rock that stuck out like a dinner plate in its side. The rock was as big as a grand piano and hung high enough above the ground to allow Eva Mae to walk upright under it. She thought it looked like a giant nose on the side of the hill. Once she got directly underneath the nose rock, she could see a big hole cut into the hill about three feet high. But when she stepped out from under the rock, it was completely unnoticeable. It was a hidden cave, obviously dug out on purpose by someone who wanted to keep it a secret.

Eva Mae stuck her head into the hidden cave entrance but it was too black to see anything. She puckered her lips and gave a quick whistle and could hear enough echo to know there was a room hidden there in the dark. She quickly decided this would be where she would camp until she could rest up. Gathering arms full of dry, dead twigs, brown grass, and dry sticks, she placed a small ring of stones under the nose rock and rubbed two carefully selected sticks together to start a small fire. It took her about a half hour to get them hot enough to start a flame, but she managed to do it. She felt proud of herself when she looked at the little fire crackling in the ring of stones. It looked just like the pictures in her outdoor camping book, and field guides. She loved to read books about nature and living in the wild.

With a small fire crackling at her feet under the nose, she made a small torch of dead moss wrapped around a small broken branch and slipped into the cave. The room lit up to reveal a ring of stones that had been used many times before for a fire, and next to it, a big pile of... familiar stuff: wetsuits, snorkels, diving masks, air tanks, and flippers. There were even underwater cameras and a harpoon. There were dozens, no, hundreds of wetsuits piled up, some old and moldy, some newer, and all were similar in size: child's sizes. Many of the suits had tears and cuts. A few of them were stained with blood and one of them kinda smelled like pee. GrumbleBriar had said that many children, mostly all boys, had come through Sirihbaz on their own journeys with the timepiece.

These must belong to all the travelers that had come before me. But who was collecting all this stuff and why did they try so hard to keep it hidden?

Eva Mae brought her sticks and fire into the cave, using the little stone ring that was already there. She failed to notice it was still warm from recent use. After she stamped out her first fire outside of the cave, she scattered the rocks and dead limbs and dirt all about the ground to cover her tracks. Slipping into the cave and lying next to her fire, she fell asleep and got the rest she so desperately needed.

The next morning came quickly and silently. There were no birds singing or rays of golden sun warming the ground. The sky just got a little less dark and the air was cool and humid. When she emerged from the cave, she grabbed the harpoon and set off to find some food. *If I can find a river, I might be able to use this harpoon to catch some breakfast.*

Her outdoor books taught her to find water by always going downhill. But the problem was that all the hills led down to the Green Heart and there was no water there, just a wall of dead, dry trees. So her only option was to climb the hill above nose rock, get a good look around, and go down the other side to find some water.

It wasn't a very high hill and the climb was pretty easy. The top of the hill gave her a better view of the Green Heart below and the ring of hills that encircled it. The forest that surrounded the ring of hills was vast and brown from a long season of drought. But off in the distance, about a mile from the bottom of the hill she stood atop, was a big field that had been cleared away of trees. In the middle of the field was a dirty little village! Most of the buildings were torn down and they were all covered in black dirt, it seemed. It looked abandoned but Eva Mae wanted to explore it anyway.

After tramping through the mile of bare branches and dead brush, she reached the village. The houses were nothing but skeletons now, with most of their walls and roofs collapsed. And they were tiny. The people that had lived here must have been very small, like children. The black dirt that covered the remains of the once quaint little village wasn't dirt at all, Eva Mae discovered. It was soot. *This village was burned! That's terrible!*

Walking through the rubble, she saw a house that still had some of its roof left, but the front wall had been broken down, revealing the room inside. She instantly noticed a pair of little brown boots sticking out from under a broken table inside. They looked as if they were on someone's feet and that they may be trapped. The boots didn't move, but it might not be too late to help. So she ran.

"Hang on!" she shouted at the boots. "I'm coming. I'll help you!"

Running up to the collapsed table, she dropped the harpoon and used both hands to lift the wooden tabletop and flip it over to free the little person's legs. She screamed when she saw that the boots belonged to a tiny skeleton, with bones burned to blackness.

Twang! Before she could think to cry out, a giant rope net sprang up around her and lifted her off the ground. The timepiece slipped out of her pocket and fell to the wood floor below.

She hung in the trap, slowly spinning and wondering what would happen next. *Who would do something like this to these little people? Who made this trap? How in the world am I going to get out of this net?* The net certainly wasn't comfortable and the more she hung there, the more uncomfortable she became. After an hour of hanging in the net, her arms and legs dangled like wet noodles and she would've fallen asleep if her empty stomach would have let her.

As afternoon approached, Eva Mae began to worry. She couldn't think of anything to free herself from the net. The knots holding it together were too tight for her to untie. She had nothing sharp enough to cut through any of the thick, hairy lines, and when she tried to use her teeth to chew on them, they tasted like moldy, wet dog hair. The smell alone was enough to make her gag.

From the edge of the forest, she heard the caw of a crow. She wriggled and twisted to turn the net so she could see what was happening. The dark bird burst from the treetops and swooped into the village. Landing on the remains of the rooftop above the net, the crow began its screechy call.

Caw-caw. Caw-caw. Caw-caw. Caw-caw. Caw-caw. Caw-caw. Caw-caw.

"Will you stop that, please?!" Eva Mae shouted with her hands over her ears. The crow just continued.

Caw-caw. Caw-caw. Caw-caw. Caw-caw. Caw-caw. Caw-caw. Caw-caw.

"STOP!" shrieked Eva Mae as she burst into tears. It was too much. She was finally afraid and felt lost. The terrible bird seemed to laugh at her. The more she cried, the happier the bird seemed.

Caw-caw. Caw-caw. Caw-caw. Caw-caw. Caw-caw. Caw-caw. Caw-caw.

"He won't listen to you," came a rough, squatty voice from below her. "He doesn't obey prisoners. You're lucky he's not pecking your eyeballs out, traveler."

"Help! Please let me down. I got caught in this net by accident. I didn't mean to do anything wrong. I thought I was helping someone," Eva Mae begged and pleaded to be freed, like a bird with its foot caught in some wire.

"An accident, eh? I think NOT." The voice was mean and sounded boastful. A little man dressed in all black, with a thick, silver beard that hung down to his knees, stepped backwards into Eva Mae's view. He was only three feet tall with fat little arms and legs, and waddled when he walked. His nose was round and he wore a little black cap.

"You're a dwarf!" Eva Mae shouted in surprise.

"Watch your mouth, child!" he snapped. "I'm a WolliPog." He slipped a knife out of its black sheath and stepped towards the net. "I'm cutting you down, but don't even think of trying to run. You belong to Braxo, now." With that, he flicked his wrist and sliced through a single line in the netting. It burst open, spilling Eva Mae to the ground. As he hurried over to grab and bind her, she stood to face him.

The WolliPog's eyes grew big and round. "You're... *a girl?!*"

"Watch your mouth, dwarf! I'm a traveler."

He quickly grabbed her wrists, tying them behind her back. "Whatever you are, you're my prisoner. And you belong to Braxo. He's been waiting for this for a long time."

Captor

The strange little man, the WolliPog, walked ahead of Eva Mae, pulling her along with a rope tied around her neck. They headed back into the forest along a dirt road. A few quick jerks from the rope and Eva Mae knew she wouldn't be strong enough to pull away from him.

Glancing back at the burnt village, she realized that the timepiece had fallen to the ground and she didn't have a chance to find it.

"Wait!" she cried. "We have to go back. I forgot my..." She remembered that this 'Braxo' guy wanted the timepiece and she didn't want to tell the dwarf exactly what she had left behind.

"... forgot, uh... something."

With a quick yank on her rope leash, the WolliPog barked, "Keep movin'! No time to waste, you little rat."

Eva Mae promised herself she would somehow manage to escape and go back for the pocket watch. Until then, her plan was to learn all she could about her captor and where they were going. After they entered the forest and had walked about a mile or so, she asked all kinds of questions.

"Why did you tie the rope around my neck? It hurts so bad. I'm not a dog, you know. Can you please tie it somewhere else?"

"No," was all the dwarf replied.

"Well, why not? I won't escape. The rope is just so itchy. And it's too tight... can you *pleeeeeeease* take it off?"

The WolliPog stopped walking but didn't turn around.

"Why don't you just stop yapping, if you're not a dog?" With that, he tugged on the rope and they continued.

They tramped through the dying forest for hours, and night would be approaching soon. The darkening clouds crackled with more lightning.

The dwarf turned his head back towards his captive and growled, "It's gonna rain soon. Perhaps I'll stop to find a place to wait until morning."

"How about the cave under nose rock! It's perfect and I know right where it's at." Eva Mae hoped the little man would let her take him there. That should get her closer to the village. She was familiar with that part of the forest now, but the farther they walked down this strange forest road, the more fearful she became.

"How about you let me decide when and where we stop?" The dwarf was getting annoyed with her constant questions and comments. "No more talking until we camp... and I speak to you first. Just keep quiet. Or else!"

"Or else, *what?*" Eva Mae defiantly replied.

The black dwarf turned around, removed the knife from its sheath again, and slowly slid the flat edge of the blade across his throat. His eyes were tired and full of anger, and his face was covered in horrible scars.

Eva Mae ignored the threat. She couldn't believe his entire face had been so scarred and she wondered how handsome he might be without them. Something about him didn't quite fit the mean, dark attitude. Sometimes, she thought the dwarf was trying too hard to act mean. He wasn't born evil, that was for sure, but something had hurt him and forced him to be this way. Eva Mae would get to the bottom of it. If there was a spark of goodness in him, she knew she could find it... and help him find it, too.

As they moved down the dirt road, the WolliPog changed course and took an abrupt left off the path and into the thick forest. Eva Mae didn't ask any questions. The dwarf moved through the forest silently ahead of her, his footsteps falling as quietly as autumn leaves. Eva Mae tried to copy the little man's stealth and placed her feet in his boot prints. She wasn't wearing any shoes and her bare feet were like the soft pads of a cat's paw. She was very proud of herself when the dwarf would suddenly turn around to make sure she was still behind him. It became a game they played, and the dwarf made no complaint about it; a couple of times, he even seemed to enjoy it. He would step quickly in a delicate, jumbled pattern then stop and wait to hear if she made any sound copying him. Sometimes she did, other times she was as silent as a fog drifting through the forest.

They walked uphill at a quick pace, but Eva Mae didn't have any problems keeping up... even with her hands tied behind her back. It was only a couple of minutes before they crested the hill and descended. At the bottom, the dwarf made another left turn and Eva Mae felt like they were backtracking.

The lightning flashed with more frequency and every so often would strike a distant tree, blackening it and lapping up its remaining life. The forest had dead, black trees peppered here and there that had been killed by the lightning. With one particularly close bolt, rain fell from the sky. It didn't slowly drizzle and build into a downpour. The rain just fell in buckets. A full shower carried by a hot wind hit their faces all at once.

"We'll stop there," the dwarf barked as he pointed his short, chubby finger off to the left. A familiar stone slab stuck out of the hillside, giving it the appearance of a giant nose.

"Nose rock!" Eva Mae shouted. "I know this place. This was what I was telling you about."

The dwarf said nothing but led her under the rock and through the hidden cave entrance. It was totally dark and while Eva Mae's eyes adjusted, she felt a sharp tug on the rope then heard the little man mutter, "Sit down." He pulled a small stone from his pocket and struck it with his knife a few times. Sparks jumped off the stone and spilled into the little fire pit. Within a minute, a warm fire crackled, giving the cave a soft glow. Plopping down on his dwarven butt, he pulled out a leather flask and took a long, slow drink.

"Ahhh." The relieved WolliPog handed the flask to Eva Mae and said, "Drink. You need water."

The girl was delighted to see that her hands were no longer bound, though the rope was still around her neck.

"Thank you," she said politely as possible, taking a long, refreshing drink of pure, cold water. After sitting in silence for quite a while, Eva Mae wanted to know more about her captor. "Where are we going?"

"Castle Mavros. I'm taking you to Lord Braxo."

"Why? What did I do wrong?"

"My Lord has been waiting a long time to capture a traveler."

"Why does he want to capture the travelers?" Eva Mae already knew that Braxo wanted the timepiece and hated the travelers, but she wanted to learn more.

"Stop being so nosey, girl!" the dwarf barked. He stared at her in silence for about a minute, then got up and tied her hands again, this time in front of her. Then he sat back down and pulled the pocket watch out of a little pouch and dangled it in front of her.

"The timepiece!" Eva Mae shrieked. "It's mine! Give it back!" She struggled to pull her hands free, but couldn't. The dwarf just laughed.

"This is what My Lord wants. And I will be greatly rewarded. Possibly even set free!" the little man said.

Set free? He must be Braxo's slave.

"How did you get all those scars on your face? Did Braxo do that to you?"

The little man's mood changed, and he sat quietly staring at the fire. After a few minutes, Eve Mae thought he would almost cry. Obviously, he greatly resented the beatings and pain that his cruel lord dealt him over countless years of slavery.

"Yes. It's the price I pay for my position."

Eva Mae didn't want to ask him any more questions. It agonized him to think and talk about his past and the pain he had to live with. With the tender compassion that only a little girl can feel, she said, "I'm sorry."

"GeriPog," the dwarf muttered. "That's my name. GeriPog. Who are you? What's your name, girl?"

"Eva Mae."

"Well, get some sleep, Eva Mae," GeriPog said as he slipped the timepiece back into his little pouch. "Tomorrow, I'm delivering you to Lord Braxo."

GeriPog quickly snuffed out the fire and crawled on top of the pile of wetsuits to watch his captive sleep in total darkness.

The Black Castle

The rain didn't stop and the next day's hike was grueling. They climbed the hill again and walked along the hilltops with the Green Heart below them to the left. They followed the ring of hills around to the other side of the forest, opposite of the burnt village and the dirt road they had taken. GeriPog said that the hilltop route was a shortcut to the castle, but it was a terrifying journey with lightning continually burning up trees, leaving much of the tops of the hills bare. Before they descended into the forest again, Eva Mae saw a tiny, black spike miles away, at the foot of a dark mountain range. GeriPog told her that the spike was Castle Mavros, their destination, and the dark range rising beyond it was the Crystal Mountains, where the WolliPog slaved day and night, mining precious magic stones for Braxo.

The walk through the dying forest was much more difficult. The ground was rocky and uneven, and thick briars and groves of dead brush caused them to weave and zigzag all day. GeriPog said nothing as he pulled Eva Mae along. She tried to play the 'silent follower' game a few times, but the dwarf didn't play along today. He was brooding and grumpy, determined to deliver his prize to Braxo, with no hint of sympathy. It was an effort for him to act as though he wasn't having second thoughts about delivering a little girl to the black wizard. He was certain that Eva Mae would be killed once the timepiece was handed over, and that he would have to find a way to live with that.

Finally, they emerged from the forest and followed the cobblestone road that ran north towards the village and south to the drawbridge of Castle Mavros. It was a black-walled castle. It wasn't black from soot or dirt or age. It wasn't painted. The stones themselves were glossy black like obsidian, each one the size of a small car. There were guard towers on each corner, and an enormous black-roofed keep in its center. From the back corner of the keep rose the tower, Braxo's tower. It was three times the height of the walls and was capped by a cone roof. GeriPog had told her earlier that day that the shingles were made from dragon scales, the last remains of an extinct species. Awhile back, when the sun would shine, before the cocoon of menacing clouds, the sunlight would reflect off the scales in dazzling colors. The tower was a glistening, shimmering beacon, inviting all to come for aid. That was before Braxo poisoned the world with his evil ambitions and dark power.

Two black-bearded WolliPogs guarded the castle entrance at the end of the drawbridge. They were both ugly, mean, and scarred. But no one was as scarred as GeriPog. The two guards had long, barbed spears and wore cone-shaped helmets. Their black tunics had a bright red crescent moon crisscrossed with a lightning bolt—Braxo's emblem. Before GeriPog crossed the drawbridge, he slipped a hood over Eva Mae's head.

"Keep quiet and do as you're told if you want to live."

As they crossed the drawbridge, the guards recognized GeriPog, stood as straight as dwarves could and raised their spears in salute. GeriPog ignored them. They were young and dumb, chosen to serve at the castle only because of their willingness to act cruelly towards animals and their own kind. They weren't picked for their strength. The strong ones were sent to the Crystal Mines for heavy labor. These were the meanest of the mean. And GeriPog was their captain, having more authority than anyone else in Braxo's empire, except the wizard himself.

As they entered the keep, Eva Mae could smell smoke and incense. It was horrible, like burning garbage and rotten fish. It was worse than a sewer, but not as strong. She tried not to gag and didn't want to learn where that nasty smell may be coming from.

"And what have you brought me today, slave?" hissed a prideful man's voice. "Another WolliPog for the mines, eh? It looks rather scrawny and tall for that." It was Braxo.

"My Lord, I bring you a *traveler!*" GeriPog announced so that all could hear. Eva Mae heard the gasps and whispers of dozens of people, or creatures of some kind. An excitement filled the room that almost sounded like panic.

"Silence!" barked Braxo. He rose from his throne and walked down the three steps to the floor in front of GeriPog. "It is true?"

"Yes, Lord. My trap in the burnt village…"

"Well done, indeed. Let's take a look, shall we?" Braxo took a few light steps past GeriPog and pulled the hood off Eva Mae. Her golden-red hair fell down over her shoulders and Braxo recoiled like a snake.

"A *girl?!*" he hissed in disgust. "This is… unexpected. A girl hasn't traveled since…" His mind drifted to the memory of his abandonment by Sarah Grankel. Braxo was visibly confused, and growing angrier by the second.

As he stared into Eva Mae's eyes, she noticed they were blood red, and his pupils weren't round, but slotted like a viper's. In a cold, mean voice, he hissed his words at her, "You disgusting little thing. Give me the timepiece." Her ropes fell to the ground, magically cut off by the wizard with a quick wave of his hand.

Eva Mae was so scared she couldn't move or speak.

"Did you hear me, you little rat? I said give it to me! It's MINE. NOW!" Braxo screamed at her. But she was frozen, shaking in fear. All she could do was look towards GeriPog, begging him with her eyes to help.

"I'll just get it myself, then..." Braxo pulled his wavy, blood-red dagger out of its sheath with one hand and grabbed Eva Mae's throat with the other. Eva Mae screamed like only an eight-year-old girl could.

"She doesn't have it, My Lord!" yelled GeriPog. Braxo stopped and slowly turned his head towards his slave. More gasps filled the room.

"Doesn't... *have* it?" the wizard hissed.

"There was another traveler with her... a boy," GeriPog lied. "I found him trying to free this one from the trap. When he saw me... he used the timepiece to escape." GeriPog had been thinking up the perfect lie all day and hoped desperately that his next words would be enough to save the girl. "The boy *abandoned his friend to save himself.*"

Braxo lowered his dagger and stepped back from the girl.

"Typical traveler scum! Leaving behind their comrades to save their own skins." Braxo spat on the floor in disgust.

It worked. The lie had distracted Braxo enough to soothe his anger and save the girl from being killed. At least for now. But Braxo wasn't pleased with the dwarf for returning without the timepiece.

"Guards!" ordered the wizard. Two WolliPog vermin stepped out of the shadows near the great double doors at the keep's grand entry. "Take this girl to the tower dungeon. She may be useful to me at some point."

As the guards moved in and seized Eva Mae by both arms, GeriPog bowed toward Braxo and said, "Please allow me, My Lord. I'm familiar with this little one's tricks. She's quite clever."

But Braxo replied, "I have a better suggestion, GeriPog." He swiftly stepped in front of the dwarf and struck him with the back of his hand. The jagged ring on the wizard's finger left a fresh, deep cut on GeriPog's face as he tumbled to the floor.

Eva Mae screamed again, "STOP!"

"Silence that little rat, guards. I'll not have outbursts like that in my keep!" At Braxo's command, the guards put a rope in Eva Mae's mouth, gagging her.

Braxo addressed GeriPog again, "My patience has run out with you, GeriPog. I gave you every opportunity to find the timepiece. And again and again and again, you come back empty handed. I took you out of the mines, thinking you could serve me. I thought you might be useful, clever, and helpful... I was clearly mistaken. You're nothing but an old, broken excuse for a slave. You're not good enough to shovel sewage in my castle." After a few seconds of reflection, Braxo decreed in a loud voice, "Go to the crystal mines and fetch me a new gem for my spells. Now get out of my site! GUARDS! Remove this WolliTrash from my castle at once!"

While Eva Mae was escorted into the dungeon beneath Braxo's tower, GeriPog was roughly dragged out by his beard and tossed off the drawbridge into the sewage-filled moat.

Yet both were still alive.

When the WolliPog climbed out of the stinky sludge and onto the bank on the other side of the moat, he rolled over on his back and stared up at the gloomy, darkening clouds. His fat little hand slid over the pouch on his belt where the timepiece was safely still tucked away. As rain fell on his face, he lay still, feeling something new and alive inside him.

He felt the *freedom to choose.*

The Green Heart

A life of slavery taught GeriPog that his only purpose in life was to do as he was told. He had never heard of a slave master asking a slave, "What would *you* like to do today?" or "What are *your* suggestions?" No. GeriPog knew that slaves were told what to do, how to think, and the manner in which they served. He was a slave and his feeling didn't mean anything to his slave master. And if he decided to have his own thoughts and feelings, he was punished, often beaten, and sometimes imprisoned. And he always believed that if he ever decided to do what he wanted to do instead of what Braxo wanted, he could be killed.

GeriPog lay on the ground, overwhelmed by the freedom to think and feel his own thoughts and feelings. His lie to Braxo saved the girl's life. And while he was banished to slave away in the mines, he now felt as though he could *choose* to run away and live his life the way *he wanted*, not how the wizard ordered. His act of bravery made him feel like he had only begun to set things right in his life. He needed to save his people. He needed to rebuild their village. But first, he needed to save his friend. She was the first person to ever show him kindness, and that one little girl was all it took to awaken the kind and compassionate WolliPog nature he was created with.

He stood and took a long look at the fortress of hate before him, and when the guards at the drawbridge looked away, he took off his boots and quietly slipped into the woods and out of Braxo's service forever.

He felt like he owned the forest as a free WolliPog. He had seen every inch of it in service to Braxo, but now he felt like it was *his home* and he was free to roam wherever he pleased. But he wouldn't casually go wherever his feet would take him. That would be nice, and he thought that maybe someday he would retire to wandering about at his leisure. But right now, he was on an errand, a quest. *His quest.* He would find help and rescue his friend, Eva Mae. He knew the castle better than anyone, even Braxo. And breaking in to rescue her would be a cinch if he had enough help. But he needed more hands and heads. He needed distractions, weapons, and something the WolliPog weren't created to do—magic.

He had the timepiece but no idea how to use it. He wasn't about to risk getting stuck in some strange world and accidentally abandon the little girl who changed him, saved him. He had to find help in Sirihbaz and decided that the base of his operations would be what Eva Mae had so adorably called "Nose Rock." It was his cave. He had dug it out years and years ago. It had been a shelter from the rain and lightning, but also became a secret place where he could hide and have his own thoughts. He had filled it with the strange, wet clothes and odd tools the travelers had left behind, and over the past several years, he had grown quite a collection. Most of it was useless junk but over a hundred of *anything* made quite an interesting collection.

As he descended the hills to the Green Heart, a stout wind picked up from the south and blew strange, salty smells. The air felt different somehow and the clouds lightened a bit. When he got to the tangled wall of Green Heart, he turned left and followed his normal path. He soon found himself under the rock that looked like a nose. He stood there under the rock facing the wall of dead, twisted trees for a while, the fresh wind soothing the new cut on his face.

A small flash of movement in the corner of his eye startled him. Something bright and colorful carried by the wind drifted alongside the Green Heart's wall. It was a fiery, red feather. GeriPog had never seen a feather so large; it was longer than an entire crow. And as it drifted closer, he could smell sulphur.

The feather blew into a tangle of branches and was stuck, ripe for the taking. But when GeriPog reached up to grab it, the wind blew it free and farther north along the wall of trees. This wasn't a prize he would easily give up on so he followed. It got caught again, inviting him to come closer, and when he did, the feather was blown free and traveled north with the wind just as before. GeriPog wondered if he wasn't supposed to catch the feather, only follow it.

He walked along the north face of the Green Heart. There were no hills that ran up from its wall here; they were rock formations and cliffs, and too high for a wise WolliPog to climb. A long time ago, he had corralled many of his own kind into this area between the wall of trees and the rocky cliffs. Braxo had been with him as they bound them all and led them away in chains. But now, he had been lured there.

The feather whipped this way and that, looping over and over, caught in what seemed like a small cyclone, before it was blown into a small opening between two entangled trees in the wall of the Green Heart. GeriPog stuck his head between to look for it and discovered he could fit his whole body through easily! He had scoured the wall many times, looking for a way into the Heart, but the twisted mass of deadwood was always too tightly entwined. Strange how he never saw this tiny gap.

The opening he crawled into became more like a tunnel, tall enough for a WolliPog or even a grown man to stand. The wind from the entrance filled the tunnel with a fresh, salty breeze that cooled him and made the tunnel hum like a low-toned flute. There were no offshoots or hallways or junctions of various passages. It was just one long tunnel that went straight to the center, a mile in. The branches above totally blocked the rain but somehow let the light in, and what really struck him was that the tunnel wasn't cut out by someone. It was naturally formed by the entangled trees.

At the center of the Green Heart, the tunnel opened into a large, empty, round room with nothing but a stone slab in the middle. Lying on that slab was the body of Green Dewin. The red feather had landed in Dewin's thick, brown beard, close to the red bloodstain on his chest. That was where Braxo had thrust his poisoned knife. GeriPog remembered the failed attempt to capture the traveler that day. The entire village was burned so that they might uncover where Dewin hid the traveler. That part was a success. But the boy was too quick for Braxo and disappeared after seeing his friend put to death. Braxo's rage against the villagers was awful. Most were killed, and slaves were made of the rest. A few had gotten away, running into the forest. GeriPog guessed that they must've come back for Dewin's body and brought it to this hidden burial chamber.

GeriPog felt a tingling, a vibrating coming from his pouch holding the timepiece, so he took it out, wondering what to do. He wouldn't use it. And keeping it in his pouch was too dangerous. This tomb was the perfect place to hide the timepiece, so he gently placed it in the palm of Green Dewin's hand.

The room lit up at once and light streamed from Dewin's eyelids. The red feather dissolved into his brown beard and the wind rushed violently into the chamber. After a few seconds more, everything stopped. The room was once again still and dark.

Dewin sat up and turned towards GeriPog, resting his feet on the dirt floor.

"Dewin!... You're... you're alive!" GeriPog had only seen magic kill and destroy. But to witness it bring life back was something beautiful, indeed.

"It would appear so," mumbled Dewin. "May I ask what brings you here? I've had enough of your trouble."

GeriPog was ashamed of himself and said nothing.

Dewin continued his scolding, "How is it that a traitor to his own people could find the nerve to enter my burial chamber and wake me, his enemy?"

GeriPog dropped to his knees. "Please, Dewin. Listen to me. I've come for your help. A traveler has been taken prisoner by Braxo."

"So, he finally caught himself a boy, eh?" Dewin looked disgusted. "Then why did he send you here? To kill me again? Once wasn't enough, eh!" Green Dewin was terrifying. The dead wood of the walls around him twisted and slithered like snakes as he shouted at the dwarf.

"No. It's a girl. The traveler is a girl."

"A girl, you say? And he let her live?" Dewin calmed a little, and the walls stopped crawling. "Tell me what happened, GeriPog."

"I trapped her in the village. I took the timepiece. But by the time we got to the castle, I... just couldn't let him have it. Just before he raised his blade to kill her, I lied to him. Told him she was abandoned by a boy who got away with the timepiece. It was enough to spare her life, for now anyways. I was banished."

Green Dewin looked down at the timepiece in his hands. "...and came to me for help, eh?"

"Please help me save her."

"We'll do nothing until this timepiece is returned to the Traveler's League," Dewin ordered. "Perhaps they will have a few extra hands to lend. We need a rescue party."

GeriPog asked how Dewin could contact the league.

"There won't be any travelers coming through here, if you have the timepiece. Are you going to use it to find them?"

"Don't be silly, GeriPog. I'd never do something that foolish. I'd get lost and most likely never return... There is another way. And you're going with me."

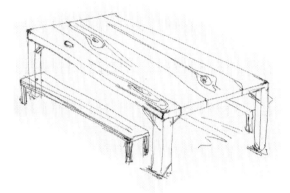

Traveler's Rest

Smitty and Toby were finishing up a game of chess. It was their twentieth game for that day.

"You know I've got you, right? You can't win." Smitty smirked. Toby was smart though, and Smitty sometimes lost to the older boy when he wasn't paying attention. Toby didn't look him in the eye. He just quietly studied the board while Smitty continued to talk trash, confident he had the victory. "Anytime you're ready to end the pain and suffering... just let me know, Toby."

Toby quietly took his knight and moved it into place. He didn't say anything at first. He just sat quietly, waiting for Smitty to realize what had just happened.

Smitty laughed too soon. "Ha. Nice try, but I've got you cornered... If I just moved this one, wait.... No. If I move *here*... no, wait, that won't work. Hold on." After about a full five minutes of silent, desperate strategizing, Smitty saw the inevitable.

"Checkmate, Captain," Toby said with his sly smile peeking from behind the curtain of black hair that swooped down over half of his face.

Smitty was angry. He was sure he had beaten Toby this time. Toby was the only member of the Traveler's League that was older than Smitty. He was fourteen years old and had more experience with the Four Gates and Five Worlds than any of the travelers on record. Smitty was thirteen and was so used to being older and smarter than almost everyone else, he sometimes forgot that even the captain of the Traveler's League could sometimes get beaten.

"Good game," Smitty relented. "I'll get you next time... The winner cleans up!" He popped up out of his seat, laughing, and walked to the storage and supplies corner for a snack. Toby put the chess pieces away and cleaned off the table. The other boys in the room were playing different games or reading. Some talked, while others wrestled and rough-housed.

The sound of the chess game box hitting the floor caught everyone's attention. All thirty-two wooden chess pieces fell to the floor, scattering all over.

"Real smooth, Toby," Smitty said over his shoulder. But Toby didn't move. He stood as still as a statue, staring at the wall. Smitty turned to look at what startled Toby, as did all the other boys in the room at the same time. The wall Toby stared at was mostly covered by a large, yellow curtain that hung from floor to ceiling. It had 'T.L.' embroidered in bold, red letters. The club of boys called it 'the Veil,' because it covered the portal embedded in the wall behind it, the portal that allowed travelers to slip directly into the Chamber of Crossroads, and from there to any of the Four Gates and Five Worlds.

Standing in front of the Veil, facing the room of boys, was GeriPog. His little black cap was in his hands, removed to show respect.

All of the boys, including Smitty, realized who the dwarf was at the same time... the evil servant of Braxo. Many of them had fought or fled GeriPog during their own journeys with the timepiece, and none of them ever expected to see him appear in Traveler's Rest. That would mean that Braxo had discovered the chamber. He wouldn't need the timepiece, creating chaos in all the other worlds.

The whole room shouted in fear and surprise at the sight of the little black villain, who just stood there. But Smitty jumped into action. He grabbed one of the swords leaning in the corner of the storage and tossed it, handing first to Toby.

"Toby, catch!" The black-haired boy turned quickly enough to snag the sword, twirl it around and stand on guard, as Smitty stepped beside him with his own blade. The two oldest boys kept their eyes on the dwarf, ready to strike him down together in a coordinated attack.

"Please. I come peacefully. I have no weapons," GeriPog shouted and held his empty arms straight out to both sides.

But the boys were too startled and distrusting to hear his words. Smitty stepped to the right with his blade pointed at GeriPog's head, while Toby circled left.

"Get on your knees, dwarf," ordered Smitty. And as the WolliPog knelt, Toby stepped behind him quietly and raised his sword. Finally, they would do it: execute Braxo's most deviant little servant. This would be a great victory against the wizard.

"STOP!" boomed a commanding voice. Toby's sword started to come down, but an icy wind blew into his eyes, freezing them shut for a few seconds, and causing him to stumble sideways. Smitty and the rest of the boys all froze at the sounds of the powerful voice. The person who owned that voice had emerged from behind the Veil and stood before them. It was Green Dewin.

"Dewin!" Every boy shouted his name at once in delight and they rushed towards him, surrounding him with great joy. One after another, they wrapped their arms around their old friend and he laughed as he returned the affection. He had comforted and assisted every single traveler who had journeyed through Sirihbaz, counting each one of them as his friend.

Only Smitty didn't run up to Dewin for a hug. He kept the tip of his sword on GeriPog's throat. He wanted to know why Braxo's little black slave was here, and what all of this meant.

"Are you all right, Toby, my boy?" Dewin lifted the teen's face in his hand to examine his eyes.

"Yeah. It's cool. I'm glad you're here. We freaked out when we saw GeriPog, though... what is he doing here, anyway?"

Dewin told all the boys to sit, which they did, except for Smitty. He stood in the middle of the room. He was ready to strike the dwarf down at the first sign of trouble, and anger made his cheeks red. Dewin grabbed GeriPog by the hand and walked over to the raised platform. He asked the WolliPog to stand on the raised wooden circle and then hushed the noisy room of boys by raising his arms.

"I'm here to ask the Traveler's League for help," Dewin began. "I would like to ask that a few brave travelers volunteer for a dangerous mission. I'm forming a rescue party." Almost every boy raised his hand and jumped up shouting, "Me! Me! I'll go!"

"The decision isn't yours or mine," Dewin told the boys and hushed them again. "Your captain must decide who will be best suited for the quest."

Smitty didn't stop looking at GeriPog, but spoke to Dewin, "Who are you rescuing?"

"A girl. She's been taken prisoner by Braxo. She is locked in the dungeon at Castle Mavros. GeriPog here, will help us slip into the dungeon, retrieve the girl and escape."

"...and then hand you over to Braxo once you're inside. Come on, Dewin! Can't you see this scarred little toad is setting you up for a trap?" Smitty was being unusually harsh. "And besides, why should we care about some random girl? Who is she? Some WolliPog slave? Why is she so important that I should put my guys in danger?"

Dewin looked at GeriPog and nodded. The dwarf reached into his pouch, pulled out the timepiece, and lifted it up as high as his fat little arms could reach, holding it by its chain.

"Because she's one of you." The room fell silent as GeriPog spoke, "She's a traveler."

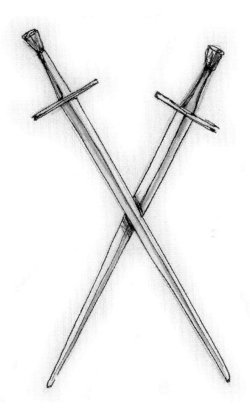

I Summon the League

"Give it to me!" Smitty ordered. "NOW!"

The sight of the timepiece in the hands of his enemy was too much for him. He was the captain of the Traveler's League. He was responsible for what happened to his boys and the pocket watch. He was a protector and a leader. So when GeriPog arrived in *Smitty's* clubhouse and held up *Smitty's* stolen timepiece, telling him that one of *Smitty's* travelers had been captured (and that she was a girl), Smitty felt like he had been made to look like a fool. He still had the sword in his hands and could feel all the other boys watching him. He became more upset second by second. His mind tried to make sense of how this all could have happened and that's when he remembered his conversation with Hoops. Hoops was the last traveler to hand on the timepiece. He had completed one of the most epic journeys on record and was a club favorite. But he had told Smitty that the Oracle of Torpil said that a girl would be the next traveler. Smitty had told Hoops that the league must always follow the 'Old Rule,' which states that only *boys* were to be chosen to travel. But Hoops clearly disregarded Smitty's instruction, and he broke the Old Rule. And because of Hoops, Smitty felt like he was made to look like a failure, the worst captain the league had ever voted for.

Smitty raised his sword high overhead and charged at GeriPog. His 'blood was boiling,' as they say, meaning he was too enraged to hear the shouts of others. When he swung at the WolliPog, he imagined he was slashing Hoops' head off.

The blade didn't reach GeriPog. It was blocked by another blade. Toby had stepped between Smitty and GeriPog at the last second.

Smitty was on fire with embarrassment and anger, and wouldn't stop his assault. He tried to move around Toby to the left, but Toby moved left too, keeping the dwarf safely behind him. Smitty jumped to the right and tried to thrust the tip of his sword past Toby, hoping to stab GeriPog. But Toby was quicker to parry the thrust with his sword. Smitty's rage completely took over and he screamed. There were no words that came out of his mouth, just the scream of a thirteen-year-old boy who had been humiliated in front of his friends. And now he was even fighting his own travelers.

Toby was on the defensive and blocked all of Smitty's thrusts and slashes. Even with his black hair swooping down over half of his face, he was the superior swordsman. He kept a cool head and didn't fight back. Keeping GeriPog safely behind him, he blocked and dodged until Smitty finally gave up in exhaustion.

Smitty wasn't the type to cry when his emotions got away from him. He was a fighter. He got angry. This time, his careless anger made him lose control, and all of the boys watching were stunned to see their trusted leader attack one of their own. The room was filled with boys, kids mostly. Toby and Smitty were the only teenagers, and it scared the boys when their leader lost control.

Catching his breath, Smitty sat on the floor and looked around the room. He knew he had failed as their leader, and that a new captain would soon be chosen. But until that happened, he had some work to do.

"I summon the league!" He stood and slowly turned, looking every boy in the eye. "Hoops has betrayed us by breaking the Old Rule. We will have a trial to vote on his banishment from Traveler's Rest."

He turned to Dewin and while he spoke to him, his eyes were stuck on GeriPog, "Tell your new dwarven slave to give me the timepiece, Dewin."

"I'm no slave, boy," GeriPog grumbled. He waddled over, keeping a close eye on Smitty's sword, and handed the pocket watch to Dewin.

"We didn't expect such a shameful welcome, Smitty," Dewin scolded the redhead. "This WolliPog made a choice to be true to his nature. He had compassion for a human girl. He lied to Braxo to save the girl's life." His voice was getting deeper and more threatening. "He came here by his own free will. Even though he was ashamed and embarrassed by the pain he had caused in the past, he felt it was right to come here."

"I don't care!" Smitty snapped. "He's my enemy... and so is Hoops."

Dewin exploded, "*You* and your cursed pride and temper are your true enemy, boy!"

Smitty recoiled in fear of the green wizard.

"You will *not* be given the timepiece. I will *not* return it to you or the league until this is sorted out."

Toby stepped in. "Dewin, if Smitty says he's sorry to GeriPog and agrees to form a rescue party, will you give him the timepiece?"

Dewin silently considered Toby's deal. He also admired the calm leadership he showed. The boys in the room all slowly gathered behind Toby. He was the only one who hadn't terrified them. Smitty and the wizard had both behaved themselves in a way that repelled the travelers. Toby was the big brother they needed in that moment.

"I'm proud of you, Toby," said Dewin in a fatherly voice. "That deal is acceptable to me. What say you, GeriPog?"

"Agreed," growled the WolliPog, eyeballing Smitty's sword.

"Smitty?" Toby put his hand on Smitty's shoulder, "Will that work for you, Captain?"

Before Smitty could answer, a series of whooshing sounds filled the clubhouse. Travelers appeared on the raised wooden platform. One by one, they would materialize, magically transported from their home world to Traveler's Rest. Whenever the league captain, whoever it may be, muttered the words *I summon the league*, the process began.

Hoops was the last to arrive. When he appeared, he wore his normal red-collared shirt and blue jeans. But he also wore the cloak that WolliTom had given him and held the magical blue knife with the white-bone handle. It was lucky for him that he was holding the knife. Smitty was ready to attack him as soon as he showed up, his sword still in his hand. But when he saw the knife Hoops held, he decided that he'd wait until a better time to take his revenge.

Hoops looked around the room and knew right away that he was in trouble. All eyes were on him and nobody was smiling. Especially Smitty.

Hoops felt like an outcast and slowly stepped off the platform without saying a word. He stared at his feet, knowing he let them down by giving the timepiece to a girl and breaking the Old Rule. He wasn't sorry for his decision. He knew it had been *the right thing to do*. And he knew he would have to answer to the Traveler's League for it eventually.

A large hand gently fell on his shoulder from behind him. Hoops spun around to a tall man in a green cloak with a long, thick, brown beard.

"Hello, my friend."

"DEWIN!" Hoops threw his arms around the wizard and pulled him as tight as he could. He couldn't help himself as tears streamed from his face. They were tears of joy and tears of regret. "I'm so sorry," he repeated again and again.

"You have nothing to be sorry for, Hoops. You did what was right. And you saved an old man." Dewin's soft and deep voice comforted the boy.

Toby said, "Welcome back, brother," then turned toward Smitty. All the other boys looked at their captain as Toby said, "The timepiece and an apology for a rescue party. Do we have a deal?"

Smitty was still angry. His pride got in the way. He would never tell GeriPog he was sorry. The WolliPog was older and wiser than anyone in the clubhouse, except Dewin, and knew Smitty couldn't get past his anger.

"I need no apology," GeriPog said in a loud voice. "I would've done the same thing, probably a lot worse. Someone would be dead for sure." The boys all laughed at the dwarf's remark. But he held up his hand to quiet them and continued, "I forgive you, Smitty. You don't have to say anything to me."

"Well, Captain?" Toby said again, "The timepiece for a rescue party?"

Smitty stood. He buried his hate deep down inside and thought *I will have my revenge.* The thought of plotting how he would get back at Hoops gave him enough willpower to pretend. He turned to Dewin and held out his hand for the timepiece.

"It's a deal."

Dungeon

The walls were slimy. The stink was incredible. It made sleeping almost impossible. This was the third day that Eva Mae had been prisoner in Braxo's dungeon. Straw was strewn across the stone floor and there was a hay bale with a blanket in the middle of the cell for a bed. A metal bucket in the corner was the toilet. Twice a day, a WolliGuard would unlock the iron door and come into the cell to deliver a plate of moldy bread and some water. The guard then took the bucket and changed it out for a new one. 'New' meant empty, not clean.

The past two nights had been full of crying. Eva Mae was lost in a world of strange and mean creatures. She had lost her timepiece and with it, all hope of returning home. She wondered about GeriPog. Braxo had sentenced him to the mines and struck him on the face. It was no wonder he was so horribly scarred, serving an evil master like that.

The girl sat on the hay bed in the cell most of the day, crying when she had the tears to do it. But when she didn't have the tears, she plotted on how she might get out. Every few hours or so, she would go to the door of her cell and call out to the guard through the iron bars. She pretended like she just wanted to talk to someone or needed more food. Really, she tried to learn about the guard and the dungeon. The more she learned, the more she schemed.

Most times, the guard either didn't answer or just barked, "Silence, toad."

Eva Mae was getting discouraged with the same old reactions from the WolliPog and thought it was time to try something different.

"Excuse me, sir? Can you hear me?" she called through the bars, "Helloooooo?"

Nothing.

She continued, "Where are you? I need a new bucket. This one is getting full.

From around a dark corner, she heard the guard grumble, "Shut up."

But she didn't shut up. "I think that WolliPogs are nothing but trolls. They stink like poop and they're uglier than dwarves."

The guard was getting irritated, "I said shut up, you dirty little roach!"

"Am I wrong? Are WolliPogs not stinky troll poop slaves? I think they are. Vicious little demon people is what you are. I bet if you turned out all the lights, a person couldn't tell the difference between the smell of your breath or your butt."

"So help me, girl... If you don't stop, I'll come in there and shut you up myself."

She continued the assault, "What do you call a candle in a suit of armor?... give up? A knight-light! Get it? *Knight* light?"

The guard moaned but she kept going.

"What do you call a cow with two legs?" This time, she waited for a response.

"Stop talking!" the WolliPog shouted again.

"Wrong!" said the girl. "Lean beef! Haha. Get it? Lean beef?"

"I get it. Now shut up, PLEEEASE!" The dwarf couldn't take much more of this. He was getting angry.

Eva Mae didn't let up. "Knock-knock."

"Shut up."

"Knock-knock."

"Stop."

"Nope. Try again. Knock-knock."

The dwarf sighed "...who's there?"

"I eat mop."

"I eat mop who?" said the guard.

"That's why your breath smells like your butt, you stinky poop troll!"

The guard had enough of this nonsense. With a grumble, he got up and waddled to the door of her cell, his keys jingling as he shoved one into the lock and pulled the door open.

Eva Mae hid by the door along the wall and out of sight. The WolliGuard walked into the room to find her.

"I'm going to break all your teeth and make you eat em' for your supper! Where are you, you little..."

Clank! Eva Mae snuck up behind the dwarf before he could turn around. She turned her toilet bucket upside down and slammed it down over the dwarf's head. It spilled all over him. As he screamed in disgust, he dropped the keys, which she quickly grabbed. She kicked the little man in the back and he fell over the hay bale bed. She ran to the door and pushed it shut. Before the dwarf could get up, she had found the right key and locked it tight.

The guard yelled and yelled. But no one could hear. Eva Mae wasn't concerned about the noise. She already knew there were no other guards in the dungeon. And there wouldn't be a new guard until tomorrow morning.

It was time to find a way out.

Rescue Party

Five shadows slipped quietly through the Chamber of Crossroads. They passed under the glowing crystal hovering twenty feet above its center. The green light reflected off their weapons. Eli had made sure they had everything they needed for a stealthy rescue. He was the Keeper of Traveler's Rest, entrusted with handling all the provisions and making sure the club was well stocked and clean. He stayed behind with Smitty, though. Most of the boys did. But Toby, Aiden, and Hoops volunteered to join the rescue party and save Eva Mae. Dewin led them through the portal at the other end of the chamber, the portal to Sirihbaz.

The Chamber of Crossroads was the great junction that connected all of the worlds of the timepiece. And in every world, there was a single hidden entrance to the chamber. If Braxo ever found out about the hidden portal in Sirihbaz, he would have no need for the timepiece. He could escape with free passage to all the other worlds.

The last to pass through the portal was GeriPog. Hoops had gone through just before him. But before he slipped through the glowing disc, he turned around to take in the wonder of this strange, domed room. Above the hovering crystal, embedded in the ceiling, was a black, swirling hole. From it, GeriPog heard all kinds of strange, horrid moans. There were screams coming from the portal in the ceiling and he instantly knew it must lead to a terrible place. A long, dark tentacle of black smoke slithered out of the portal above and slowly snaked its way towards the WolliPog. Frozen with fear, GeriPog could only watch as it got closer.

"*GeriPog,*" a pair of voices hissed. But before the smoke got to him, Dewin's arm reached back through the portal, grabbed him by his shirt collar and pulled him through.

"What in the Five Worlds was *that!*" the WolliPog gasped.

"The twin shadow wizards," Dewin said. "Malek and Trollkarl. They're imprisoned in the chamber. We must always pass silently and quickly when we travel through that powerful place." Dewin stopped and made sure everyone was listening. "We must NEVER speak their names in the Chamber of Crossroads."

Nobody asked why. It was understood that only something terrible could happen if the rule was broken. With the speaking of their ancient names, they could be released. "Their very names are ancient spells. Powerful and destructive."

The portal to Sirihbaz was in Dewin's burial chamber, embedded in the wall of an earthen room that had been dug out from under the stone slab that Dewin's body had been resting on. The rescue party slid the big, flat piece of stone off its base and climbed out into the wooden chamber.

"We will rest here while we formulate the details of our plan," Dewin ordered. "A little light, if you please, Aiden."

Aiden slid his backpack off and pulled out a small, green crystal. It was the size of a golf ball. When the scrawny boy handed it to the wizard, Dewin gently blew on it and waved his hand over it. The stone began to shine with a warm light that filled the room. Toby and GeriPog lifted the stone slab back onto its base, making a table, around which they pieced together a plan to free their fellow traveler.

The Plan

"You have got to be kidding me!" Aiden didn't like how the plan was being laid out. "The sewer? Are you crazy?"

GeriPog reassured the scrawny boy, "It's the only way into the dungeon that is unguarded. You three boys should have no trouble swimming right up under her cell."

Toby wasn't excited about the plan either. "GeriPog may be right, but there *has* to be an easier way in. Dewin, can't you just use some kind of fog spell? If the whole castle is fogged up, GeriPog could lead us right in, undetected."

GeriPog reminded him that getting out would be the real challenge, especially if they were detected and had to fight their way out. Nobody would follow them into the sewer and it would give them enough of a lead to escape into the woods. Once they were in the woods, Dewin the green wizard could hide and protect them.

"I don't see how we can swim in a moat of sewage and into the underwater tunnels. How long will we have to hold our breath? And how will we even be able to see with stinky poop and pee water in our eyes?" Hoops gagged just thinking about it.

GeriPog smiled and said, "Already thought about that, boy." He told the group to pack up and led them out of the chamber. When they emerged from the Green Heart's wall of trees, he guided them to the hidden cave under nose rock.

Dewin illuminated the cave with his glowing green stone and the three boys gasped. A giant pile of diving gear lay before them.

"I see you like my collection. You travelers sure do have some strange gear." GeriPog held up a diving mask.

Hoops dug through the heap of air tanks and added, "A lot of these tanks still have hours of oxygen left! And the masks and mouthpieces will keep the sewage out of our eyes and mouths."

"Hoops," Toby was serious looking. "We'll need to find a full set of gear for the girl. But you're the only one who knows what she looks like. We need you to set aside anything that might be her size."

"You got it, Captain... I mean, Toby."

Hoops and Aiden already thought of Toby as their leader. Smitty had failed to control himself and lost the trust of many of the boys.

Toby corrected Hoops immediately, "I'm nobody's captain! Just trying to think through this thing." He turned towards Dewin and asked, "When do we go to the castle?"

Dewin explained the timing of the rescue to them. They would have to wait another three days before they could sneak into the dungeon.

"As you boys know, Braxo casts his spell to gaze into the other worlds, looking for the timepiece. But he can only do it when the Torpil moon is full... when the moon reaches its peak in the sky."

"That means midnight. You boys will have to swim in absolute darkness." GeriPog grinned from ear to ear. He was glad he hadn't been chosen to sneak in through the sewer.

Dewin continued, "Braxo's mind will be in another world. Aiden will dash into the woods east of the castle and set beacon fires. That should be enough to distract the WolliGuards, and if all goes according to plan, we'll be able to rescue the girl right out from under Braxo's nose. When the moon wanes, the spell will break, and we should be far into the forest by then. With a little luck, we will be in Traveler's Rest before Braxo realizes she's gone."

Roaming the Tower

Eva Mae kept to the shadows. She slipped past the WolliGuards that stood post at the entrance of the dungeon. They were lazy and inattentive. A simple tossing of a stone was enough to get them to move from their posts. She snuck into the long, dark hallway that wound its way around the base of Braxo's tower and into the keep. When she stood at the archway and peered into the keep, she recognized that horrid smell again. *It must be the moat. I think if I can get across the room, and through those big double doors, I can escape outside.*

The keep had a colonnade that lined its walls. Eva Mae tiptoed from column to column, stopping in the shadow of each to wait and listen. There was no one around. The room appeared empty except for the throne on one end of the great room, and the smell, of course. Only two more columns until she was at the doors. Her plan was to somehow get through them without alarming the WolliGuards that stood just outside. She also had to think about how to get past the two ugly dwarves at the drawbridge.

She had been out of her cell for a couple of hours now. She was very careful not to move or make any noise. But that meant being still for a long time and Eva Mae wasn't very good at staying still. It was torture to stand like a statue, straining to listen for any sounds that might be approaching guards. And the smell made standing still worse. She just couldn't get used to it. Three days ago, she was brought to the castle and the smell still made her stomach turn. Every breath was filled with the stink of the moat.

Her goal was to reach the forest. She had been blindfolded by GeriPog before they had crossed the drawbridge. But she knew that if she could only reach the trees on the other side of the moat, she could find her way back. Her sense of direction was excellent. In fact, it was better than all of her friends, boys and girls alike. Even in this strange world where the sun was constantly blocked by clouds, and the stars were hidden at night, she always knew when she was headed north. She knew that the great iron doors at the keep's entrance faced north.

Finally, she reached the great double doors, but they were too heavy for her to open. Her little hands yanked and pulled on the giant iron rings, but the massive doors wouldn't budge.

Dang it. I'll have to find another way outside or wait here for the guards to open these stupid doors.

She quietly slipped from column to column, exploring the borders of the room. The doors that led to the dungeon were in the western wall of the room, and great double doors to the drawbridge were on the north wall. The eastern wall had no openings or doors at all. It ran all the way back to the south end where Braxo's throne sat on a raised platform. But behind the throne, in the south wall was a small archway. There was no door, just an opening tall enough for a man to walk through without bumping his head, but no taller.

Eva Mae stuck her head through the archway to check for guards. There was no one in either direction. But there were steps. To the right of the doorway ran a stone staircase that went up and around the base of the tower. Along its wall, every several yards, hung ensconced torches. *Too much light. I'll never be able to hide if someone comes down the stairs.* Looking in the other direction, Eva Mae saw nothing but black. She couldn't tell if the hallway ended at a door, or a staircase, or a dead end. It was just black. *I guess that's where I must go.*

As she stepped into the hallway and looked up the stairwell, a squatty, mean voice shouted from the shadows behind her, "Who goes there!" A guard had been standing post in the hall's dark shadow.

Eva Mae panicked. She bounded towards the lit stairs and began to climb. The steps wound up and to the right in a long, unending climb. The sound of the guards jostling towards her kept her mind off how tired she was getting. She was a lot faster than the dwarves and could bolt up the steps quickly at first, gaining a good lead. But the stairs just kept on going and going. There was never a door to slip through, or a landing to briefly rest on. Her only choices were to keep climbing or get caught by the WolliGuards and thrown back into her cell.

After a couple more minutes of sprinting up the stone steps, her legs felt like they were on fire and she was out of breath. Finally, the stairs ended. At the top of the winding staircase was a single, wooden door, left open. She tumbled through the open doorway and slammed it behind her. It locked on its own, with a clicking sound inside the wood. The guards arrived and pushed and banged on the door, shouting at her. But they couldn't get in.

As the mean little dwarves sounded the alarm throughout the castle, Eva Mae looked about the room to find a place to either escape through or hide in. But there was none. The room was a round chamber, with no windows, doors, or columns. Torches lined the walls, giving them a pale orange glow. But the middle of the room was gray. A raised, circular platform, two steps high, lay in the center. In the middle of the platform as a block of glossy, black stone, just like the ones used to construct the walls of the castle. Atop the black stone was a dark-purple chunk of crystal. It had no particular shape and was about the size of a dwarf. Eva Mae was captivated by the purple gem and slowly stepped up onto the platform. She carefully reached out to feel the crystal.

"Isn't it beautiful?" a man's voice hissed from behind her. Eva Mae spun around to see Braxo strolling towards her from across the room.

"It contains magic," he continued. "This one is perfect for my spell. It came from the deepest, darkest cavern in the mountains. It's ancient."

Eva Mae didn't know what to say. She stepped back and looked frantically about the room for any place she might run.

"There's no place to go," hissed the wizard. "Please, have a seat. Be my guest." Eva Mae felt invisible hands grab her by the arms and force her into a chair that appeared out of nowhere.

The guards were still banging on the door and the noise began to annoy Braxo. He turned his head towards the door and nodded. The door unlatched and burst open. Five WolliGuards tumbled over each other onto the floor.

One of them spoke as he sprang to his feet, "My Lord, I spotted this one in the great hall. She's escaped somehow. Shall I take her back to her cell?"

Braxo was amused by the whole thing, "Oh? She escaped? How clever of you to notice."

"Thank you, My Lord." The dwarf had no idea he was being mocked.

"No. Leave her here with me," Braxo ordered. "You may return to your post. All of you." He walked up to Eva Mae's chair and took her by the chin. His eyes were like a viper's, slotted and red, as if a snake walked around in a man's skin.

"She is our guest... we have much to discuss."

First Lesson

"Balance is a myth, you see..."
Braxo continued. He'd been talking
nonstop about the magical condition of
Sirihbaz. His resentment ran deep, and he
took the opportunity to seek sympathy
from anyone who would listen. Now, he
had a girl from another world to share his
story with. He didn't know she was a

traveler. He thought that she, like him, had been betrayed and abandoned.

"Only fools who have no ambition seek balance. I'm no fool, girl. My destiny is to rule the Four Gates and Five Worlds. But it will not be from this pee-infested swamp of a world."

Braxo went on about the other worlds he had seen. He had never been to these worlds, but he had seen them through the eyes of their creatures.

"Every month, when the Torpil moon is at its zenith, I cast a most delectable spell. It takes me to whatever world the timepiece is in and gets me close to it. I discover who has it and see the inner workings of their world. I've been everywhere. I've even seen your world, girl."

Eva Mae was still afraid, but not too afraid to think or talk back to the wizard, "So, you're trapped here?"

The wizard hissed back at her, "Not for long. My escape from this miserable forest is imminent. Your friend should be finishing up his travels with the timepiece soon. And the next boy to pass through Sirihbaz will be mine."

Braxo moved towards the podium with the crystal mounted on top. When he moved, he glided across the floor as if slowly sliding on ice. The black cloak he wore made a slithering sound as he moved. There were no footsteps to be heard. He placed his hand on the block of purple crystal.

"I was about your age when I was abandoned. I fell into a ravine in the Crystal Mountains. My legs were crushed from the fall, and I lay there in agony for days."

"I'm sorry." Eva Mae couldn't stand the thought of a boy being in that kind of pain.

Braxo ignored the girl's compassion. "That's where I discovered these stones." He turned and set his snake eyes on her. "Come here. I want you to feel the power of the stone."

Eva Mae had no interest in the wizard's dark magic. "That's okay," she whimpered.

"I said, *come!*" The girl was lifted a few inches off the chair by invisible bony hands, and she floated towards the wizard. She was placed on her feet next to him.

"Give me your hand." Braxo roughly grabbed her wrist. "Now place it on the stone. Yes. Like that."

Resisting the wizard's invisible strength was impossible for an eight-year-old girl. She placed her hand on the crystal as instructed.

He continued, "Now stretch out your other hand towards the chair."

She did as instructed again.

"Use the stone's power to wrap your hand around it. Use your mind to imagine it being crushed. Feel the wood with your fingertips and let your anger do the work."

Eva Mae looked past her outstretched arm at the chair. It vibrated a few inches off the floor. It shook like an earthquake was directly underneath it.

Braxo's eyes widened with pleasure, "Yessss. Good. Keep going. Think of your friend abandoning you. Think of your pathetic waste of a life in your world. Think of the betrayal. The pain."

A sharp cracking sound filled the chamber as the chair crumpled into a mass of splinters. Eva Mae couldn't believe it and was terrified that such power had flowed through her.

Braxo laughed and clapped his hands like a baby in front of a birthday cake. "Excellent. Good. You have power, girl. Great power. It feels good, doesn't it?"

Eva Mae whimpered fearfully, but the wizard ignored her remark. He glided over to the broken planks and examined them. Turning to her again, he instructed her to reach out again, "Now, lift the heap of wood and cast it across the room. Go on."

Eva Mae reached out again, but she didn't summon her anger. Braxo was irritated that nothing happened. "No. No.

You must hate it. You can't just stick your arms out in the air. The power flows through your anger. Try it again, girl."

She didn't want to do this anymore. She was tired and afraid.

"Again!" Braxo barked but Eva Mae didn't move. "You disappoint me, little one." An invisible bony hand slapped her across the face. Her cheek stung from the blow and she began to cry.

"I said, *again!*"

Eva Mae's anger welled up in her little heart. She wouldn't obey the wizard. In defiance, she turned and placed both hands on the crystal and shoved it off its pedestal. When it fell to the stone floor, it shattered into thousands of crystalline shards.

"NO!" Braxo cried out in a panic.

Eva Mae turned to the wizard with her jaw clenched tight and tears in her eyes.

The wizard's eyes pulsated with anger for only a moment. He called out, "GUARDS!"

The door to the chamber flung open and the five little dwarves hobbled in.

"Take the prisoner back to her cell at once. No food for three days... and bring me another stone!" He turned his viper eyes to the girl. "I'll teach you to obey me. I expect better behavior from you, my little apprentice."

As the guards approached her, she yelled, "I'll never be your apprentice! I'd rather die!"

Another invisible slap sent her to the ground crying. Braxo didn't say a word. He only nodded to the guards who began to pick Eva Mae off the ground.

They didn't see the small crystal shard she slipped into her pocket.

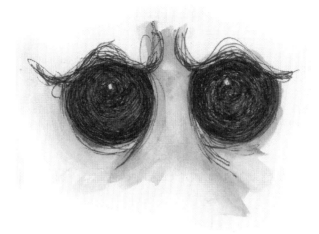

The Torpil Spell

Braxo held his blood-red dagger overhead. A partition in the dragon-shingled, cone roof had been flung open. Torpil, the oracle moon, had risen to its peak and was full again, allowing him to perform his dark work. The clouds dissipated briefly when the moon was full, and the forest would grow silent. The constant barrage of thunder and lightning would cease for only one hour as the power of Torpil calmed and illuminated the midnight sky.

With both hands on the handle of the knife, the black wizard closed his eyes and muttered the words to the spell. A piece of dark crystal was embedded in its hilt, and the crimson steel of the blade was tainted with the blood of innocents. It was a powerfully wicked knife. Braxo had gone through great lengths to have it forged... and cursed. When he embedded the crystal in its black handle, he dedicated its work to the dark arts, invoking the names of Malek and Trollkarl. They were the ancient shadow wizards, now powerful dark spirits.

When he spoke the final word of the spell, he thrust the red blade into a new block of dark crystal. With an army of WolliPog slaves mining the Crystal Mountains, Braxo had an unending supply of magic stones. A tiny spark deep within the purple, crystalline block flickered, and when he opened his eyes again, they were solid-black, inky orbs.

*****

A redheaded boy sat alone in the corner of a clubhouse. He was brooding. Something was delightfully wrong with him, and he sat in a dark cloud of glum awkwardness. The other boys in the room tried to avoid him. Braxo recognized almost every face. He even knew their names. The mind of the boy he had taken control of revealed much to him.

I'm in Traveler's Rest! Braxo thought. Excellent. Now where is the timepiece, I wonder?

Braxo looked through the eyes of another boy who had been digging through boxes and crates, surrounded by checklists and journals. *Eli.*

He moved cautiously through the room, taking care not to look any boy in the eyes. That would give him away. Many of these boys knew that if a creature had black eyes, it meant Braxo had control of that being's mind and will. Any of these boys could have the timepiece, but the redhead in the corner interested him the most, so he started there.

He sat across from Smitty and straddled the bench, leaning his back against the wall. Hanging his head, he pretended to make notes in a journal as he struck up a conversation.

"Are you hungry, Peter... er, Smitty?" Braxo almost forgot that many of the boys used nicknames.

"Bug off, Eli!" Smitty snapped. "Go serve your friends."

"Aren't you my friend, too?"

"I saw you standing behind Toby and Hoops. I know you don't want me to be captain anymore." Smitty was a fiery little brat.

Braxo looked around the room for Worthington. Hoops was the nickname his friends had given him. And he was the last one Braxo had seen with the timepiece. Three times he had seen Worthington with it. First in the jungle through the eyes of a grouchy beast. The second time, he found him hiding in Dewin's home, just outside the WolliPog village. Braxo smiled as he remembered burying his blade in the green wizard's chest. The third time, he almost wrestled the pocket watch free from Worthington's hands in the Labyrinth. That cursed minotaur ruined everything, though.

Hoops was nowhere to be seen in the clubhouse, neither was Toby the Retriever. Braxo hated Toby more than any other traveler. He had seen him dozens of times. Slipping from world to world, fighting and evading capture and death with ease. *If I ever get a chance to put my hands on Toby, I'll gut him like a fish and bathe in his blood.*

"What are you smiling at?" Smitty barked at him. "Can't you just leave me alone?"

Braxo didn't realize he was making Eli smile as he imagined killing Toby.

"So, tell me again where did *the dog* and his boy run off to, *Captain?*" Braxo said as gently as he could. He wasn't good at compassion but was a master of deception.

"You saw them leave with Dewin. They volunteered to be a part of that stupid rescue party. As captain, I don't think it's right to risk our best travelers to take on some suicide mission. Hoops broke the Old Rule, and now we have to save some stupid *girl.*"

"The Old Rule," repeated Braxo, "...of course. How dare he. I can't remember the exact words. Maybe I wrote it down in this journal." Braxo flipped through the pages, pretending to search. The rustles of the papers and acting like he was disorganized and ignorant was enough to irritate Smitty into giving him what he wanted.

"No traveler shall at any time relinquish the timepiece on his last mission to a girl. It has been decided by the Traveler's League that henceforth only boys shall be chosen to adventure with the timepiece and be eligible for membership in our league. Douglas Escobar, captain presiding over Council XVIII."

Eli looked sideways at Smitty, who hung his head as he mumbled the words to the Old Rule.

"So. The girl was the traveler," he hissed in fury.

The airy hissing sound of Eli's voice caught Smitty's attention, and his head snapped up. He stared into the black inky orbs that only moments ago were Eli's eyes.

"Braxo!" he shouted in both disgust and surprise. He jumped across the table in a flash, taking Eli to the ground. Other boys ran over to pull him off as he violently attacked the Keeper, throwing punch after punch. But Smitty straddled the boy's chest and landed his fists on Eli's nose several times, breaking it. But Eli didn't resist or fight back. *He laughed.* As Smitty punched him in the face, Braxo's laughter filled the clubhouse. The rest of the boys dogpiled on Smitty and pulled him off the Keeper. One boy grabbed Eli's arm and pulled him to his feet, but his eyes had returned to normal and he cried from the pain of his broken nose. The blood ran down his shirt as he scowled at the captain.

"What are you doing, Smitty? Are you crazy?! Get away from me!" Eli yelled.

Smitty said nothing. His blood was still hot, and he was breathing heavily as several boys held him back.

*****

Braxo opened his own eyes and gazed up at Torpil through the roof of his tower. *GeriPog lied to me... the girl was the traveler. I was a fool.*

He paced back and forth across his chamber as he thought about how to deal with the rescue party that would be arriving soon to save the girl. *She obviously doesn't have the timepiece. Someone in Traveler's Rest had it. No one in this 'rescue party' has it either... how are they getting into Sirihbaz? And how will they escape?* It was a mystery to Braxo, and he vowed to solve it.

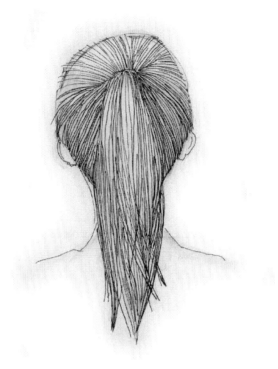

A Girl Worth Saving

It took all of Toby and Hoops' strength to lift the metal grate overhead and slide it off to the side. They were exhausted from a horrific swim in the sewer. They climbed out of the tunnel and sat for a moment to catch their breath. Hoops tore his mask off and retched from the smell of the water covering his wetsuit. Toby didn't gag, though. He threw up his lunch.

They were in a dungeon washroom, just like GeriPog had promised. Metal buckets were stacked in the corner, chains and manacles were piled up on the floor, and an empty, bloodstained table were the room's only contents. GeriPog had gone over the layout of the dungeon with Toby several times to ensure he could get to the girl's cell in the dark. But the most challenging part of the mission wasn't finding the cell or dealing with the guards. It was the swim. Toby was a little worried about getting the girl out through the sewer now that he had experienced it firsthand.

"That was the grossest thing I've ever seen, Hoops. Do you think the girl will make it? What do you know about her?"

"I have no idea. But I don't think she'll have a choice." Hoops knew very little about the girl he had given the timepiece to. She was perky and chipper, he remembered. And she seemed to like a good challenge. Hoops felt like she could do anything that he could, from the brief encounter at the playground.

"Well," Toby said after catching his breath, "only one way to find out. Let's get going. Ready?"

"Ready."

GeriPog had told them that two WolliGuards stood post outside the door of the dungeon. But the washroom was in the hallway that led to the cells, well inside the dungeon and away from its entrance. If all went according to plan, and they were quiet, they would only have to deal with the dungeon keeper, who sat in the main room that connected all the cells. They needed to distract and immobilize him without raising an alarm. After that, they could take his keys, release the girl, and escape through the washroom sewer grate.

Hoops had stuffed his cloak into his wetsuit before they left. He pulled it out, gave it a good shake, and tossed it to Toby.

"So how does this thing work again?" Toby had never used this particular magic item before. He was no stranger to magic but didn't want to assume anything.

"When you slip the hood of the cloak over your head, you'll go invisible," Hoops reminded him. "It's really not that hard to figure out, genius."

"Everything is harder than it seems, Hoops." Toby had been in enough sticky situations to know that even the simplest actions seemed difficult and uncoordinated when under pressure. That was the wisdom of experience. That was why Toby was a part of the rescue party.

Hoops slowly pulled the door open that led into the hallway. The soft creaking of the wood on its hinges didn't alarm the guards outside the entrance, but did get the attention of the keeper down the hall.

"Who's there?" he barked as he grabbed a torch and waddled down the hallway. Hoops left the door open and hid behind it while Toby tied the cloak around his shoulders and pulled the hood over his head. He disappeared just before the keeper walked into the washroom.

The keeper's torch lit the walls and the floor. The keeper suddenly noticed the grate in the floor had been removed and pushed to the side. But before he could call out to the guards, he was knocked unconscious. A single blow by an invisible boy was enough to send the keeper to the ground. Toby pulled the hood back and reappeared, holding his sword. He had used the steel pommel of the handle to knock the guard out.

"Quick, Hoops. Tie him up and gag him." Toby kept watch as Hoops tied the keeper's wrists behind his back and then put a gag cloth in his mouth.

"Do you want to hit him again to make sure he doesn't wake up too soon?" Hoops wasn't used to this kind of violence.

"I'll keep an eye on him... and the entrance. Grab his keys and get the girl. And don't take too long. This place gives me the creeps."

Hoops removed the keys from the keeper's belt and tiptoed down the hallway to the cells. There were five cells in the dungeon. Four of them were empty. But when Hoops peeked through the bars in the fifth cell's door, he found Eva Mae. She sat on a bale of dirty hay. She had one hand stretched out in front of her, and her other hand was in her lap, clutching a glowing purple stone. On the other side of the room, a metal bucket hovered three feet off the ground. *She was using magic!*

Hoops tried each key on the keeper's keychain, and as his luck would have it, it was the last key that fit the lock to the girl's cell. When the door opened, he stepped into the cell to find the girl sitting just as before but the bucket was on the floor, and the stone was nowhere to be seen.

"Eva Mae," he whispered. "Do you remember me?"

"Hoops!" she shrieked in surprise. The sound of her high-pitched voice bounced off the cell walls and down the hallway.

"SHHHH! Be quiet. We're here to get you out." Hoops was nervous about the guards hearing the noise.

Eva Mae ran to him to hug him but when she got close, she noticed the smell of his wetsuit. "Ew, gross. I didn't think the smell in here could get worse!"

"Yeah. Sorry about that. Come with me. We have a way out of here."

"Who's with you?" Eva Mae asked. But Hoops didn't answer. He led her by the hand out of the cell.

A shout came from down the hallway, "What's going on down there? RattlePog! What was that noise?" Two WolliGuards, side by side, walked slowly down the hallway towards the cells. Their spears were lowered. They had heard the girl's voice and knew something was up. Halfway down the hallway, they realized the girl had been released and a boy attempted to rescue her.

One of the guards shouted, "Hold it right there." They had their spears pointed at Hoops and the girl as they approached. But before the first guard could tell his comrade to go for help, he gasped and gurgled as the tip of a sword suddenly popped out of his chest. As he fell to the ground, Toby removed the hood of the cloak. He had thrust his sword through the dwarf's heart from behind him. The other guard turned and ran. He was too quick for Toby and ran towards the dungeon entrance.

"Quick, Toby! He's getting away!" Hoops shouted, but the guard was too fast to catch.

Suddenly, the guard's spear dropped to the ground, and he stopped running. He grabbed at his own throat as he was lifted three feet off the floor by an unseen force. Hoops turned around to see Eva Mae with her hand stretched out towards the guard. In her other hand was the glowing purple stone.

Toby wasted no time and quickly thrust his sword through the hovering dwarf's chest.

"We've got to go," Toby ordered as he slipped into the washroom. "Now!"

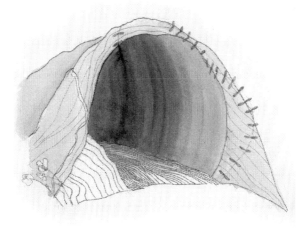

Darkness and Betrayal

Whoosh.

The air was dry and cool. But it was still. Total darkness shrouded the world when Smitty opened his eyes. He knew where he was, and it was exactly where he intended to travel. He was careful not to let any of the other boys see him set the timepiece to three o'clock. He hated them. They turned their back on him when he attacked Eli. He tried to explain that Braxo had taken over the keeper's mind, but they didn't believe him. He hated them for that, too. Or maybe they turned their back on him when he lost his temper and dueled with Toby. He knew they all secretly wished Toby was their captain. Just one more thing for Smitty to hate about the boys in Traveler's Rest. After all his adventures and all his work serving as their captain, he felt betrayed. He felt abandoned.

I have the timepiece now. Curse them all! Let them come and get it.

Smitty stood and brushed unseen dirt from his pants. He gave a quick whistle to listen for where the echo might come from in the cave. With only a few dozen steps, he saw an orange light washing the cave wall from around a corner. When he rounded the corner, he emerged from the mouth of the cave, surprised that a campfire was still burning. A pile of deadwood was on fire in the center of a ring of stones.

Hoops never put the fire out. I wonder how long it's been burning? Stupid fool. Smitty kicked one of the stones from the ring. The pile of burning sticks shifted and collapsed to one side.

An icy wind blew over his left ear for only a second. It was an odd change in the air and it stopped as quickly as it had begun. The air was perfectly still once more, and the redhead wondered what else might be in the shadow realm with him. This was his sanctuary, his solitary hiding place. He came here to be alone, away from the travelers and from the judging eyes of people who thought too highly of themselves. Now, it felt like there was a presence nearby. Something was watching him, he was sure of it. Or maybe it was *someone*.

Another icy wind from the cave whisked across his other ear. There was something in there for sure. But he wasn't fearful. His temper always fired up before his fear did. He grabbed a nearby stick from the desert floor and thrust the tip of it into the fire. When he pulled it out, it made a perfect torch. His experience in this world had taught him that fires didn't go out on their own, and that objects never stopped burning once they were lit.

Smitty marched through the cave's entrance without caution.

"Who's there?" he demanded. He waved the torch back and forth for any signs of movement. "Show yourself!" His voice echoed to the back of the cave but no one answered.

From the shadows deep within the mountain, the icy wind burst towards him and snuffed out his torch. Darkness surrounded him once again, but this time, his heart raced just a little bit faster.

"*Petros o Magos...*" a pair of thin ancient voices whispered from the blackness, their breath caused frost to form in his red hair.

He stumbled backwards, tripping over his own feet and falling to the ground. In a panic, he crawled out of the cave, kicking up dirt from his hands and knees. He stood next to the fire and stared into the cave, wondering what or who was in there.

There was no doubt he was afraid, but his fear fueled his temper even more. He snatched up two sticks this time and lit them. With a torch in each hand, he was ready to confront the visitor in the darkness. He stood before the cave and held his fiery weapons out to his sides.

"I'm coming in, so you'd better be ready. You don't know who you've messed with!" It was the best he could come up with as he tried not to sound afraid.

As he stepped into the cave, the icy whispers beckoned him again, "*Petros o Magos...*"

He stood still for a moment, second guessing his decision to enter the darkness. The voices floated out of the cave again, "*Come and see...*"

He held his torches in front of him, ready to strike anything that moved, then he took slow steps through the cave's mouth.

"*Come... Follow... Come and see...*" the voices whispered over and over. Each time farther back into the belly of the mountain. Smitty followed, his temper and his sense of adventure overriding his fear and better judgement.

In the deepest part of the mountain, Smitty stepped into a small cavern. As he ran the torches along the walls, he illuminated the mural of black sketching and ancient pictographs. They were sinister writings in ancient languages. Magical symbols and strange spells surrounded a large drawing of two black serpents. They were intertwined as their bodies formed a large circle. Within the circle was a giant, slotted, black eye, like a snake's. The flames of his torches reflected off the eye's black paint. For a moment, the eye seemed to be alive.

"*Name us,*" the icy whispers pleaded as Smitty stared at the ancient image. Smitty studied the inscriptions on the walls and ignored the airy requests. The light from his torches revealed texts that seemed to go on forever. There were writings in all kinds of different languages, some he recognized, but most he did not. They all seemed to repeat the same two words, each time in a different language. Finally, he came to a pair of words written in letters he recognized. He didn't know the earthen language, but he sounded out the letters as he tried to read them.

"Ma... Lek."

A frosty breath repeated him, whispering the name directly into his left ear. "*Malek...*"

The hairs on the back of his neck stood on end. It was the eeriest feeling he'd ever had, but he kept reading. This was an ancient secret, a powerful forgotten force. Smitty felt like he had been chosen to uncover it after lying dormant and hidden for centuries.

"Troll... Karl," Smitty continued.

Another icy breath in his right ear repeated the second name. "*Trollkarl...*"

His whole body suddenly felt cold with terror as the torches were blown out.

Catching Up

When Eva Mae rose to the surface, Toby grabbed her arm and pulled her up onto the bank. Hoops was right behind her. They ripped the wetsuits from their bodies and tore off their masks and breathing pieces. Then they kicked the pile of stinky mess, flippers and all back into the sewage-filled moat.

The sky to the east, on the opposite side of Castle Mavros glowed. A dark-orange haze washed over the horizon just above the trees of the dead forest. It wasn't the light dawn. The party had climbed out of the moat no later than one a.m. and the sun didn't rise that early.

"What's that? What's going on?" Eva Mae asked.

"That's our distraction," Toby informed her. "No time to lose. Let's go."

Toby led the way into the forest to the west. There was no path or trail to follow, and Toby was careful to follow Dewin's instructions to the letter.

"Head due west into the forest. Avoid roads and pathways. When you come to a river, follow it to the north. GeriPog and I will catch up to you," Toby recanted Dewin's words to the other two.

"Did you say *GeriPog?*" Eva Mae asked. "I know him! He's the one who saved me! He should have my timepiece. We'll be able to use it to get out of here!"

"GeriPog doesn't have the timepiece, Eva Mae. He and Dewin handed it over to the Traveler's League," Toby explained. "It was part of the deal."

"Deal?" There was a lot Eva Mae didn't know, "What deal? And what's the Traveler's League?"

Hoops spent the next hour explaining how GeriPog found Dewin, how they went to Traveler's Rest, saw the fight between Toby and Smitty, then finally made a deal to trade the pocket watch for a rescue party. Eva Mae asked about the Old Rule, and Hoops told her how he thought it was a stupid rule, and that the timepiece chose who should travel next.

"The Oracle told me that only a girl could defeat Braxo and save Sirihbaz. But when I went on my last mission to find the next traveler, I had been warned by Smitty not to give the timepiece to a girl."

"I don't think I like this *Smitty* kid very much. He sounds mean," Eva Mae said.

"He's just proud," Toby interjected. "He's been a good captain. We all really liked him at first. But he liked being captain more than most of the boys before him. When he lost his temper in front of all of us, he embarrassed himself, and his pride got the better of him."

When Eva Mae asked Hoops how the timepiece had chosen her, he said his second shadow appeared and directed him.

"That's weird!" Eva Mae said. "*TWO shadows?*"

"Yeah. I know, right?" Hoops said.

Hoops and Eva Mae talked about their travels as they walked side by side. Toby led the way silently, keeping a close eye out for any signs of danger.

Eventually, they came to a riverbank and made a hard right, following the river north as Dewin had instructed.

Eva Mae told the boys, "I've heard of Dewin. The old tree told about him. He said that Dewin had planted him and used his magic to keep the forest beautiful."

"A *tree* told you that?" Toby wasn't buying it.

"Yep."

"Trees don't talk."

"Yes, they do. Some of them," said Eva Mae.

Hoops asked, "What else did the tree tell you?" He was excited to learn something new about Sirihbaz. He had experienced so much already, more than most travelers. But he never met a talking tree.

"His name is GrumbleBriar. And he told me the story of Braxo and how a girl left him here..."

"... Sarah Grankel?" Hoops asked.

"I think that was her name, yeah. And Braxo's real name is actually *Bradford!*"

They all laughed when she said *Bradford*. The thought of a black wizard with such a common, innocent-sounding name was funny, like if the King of England's name was Barry.

As they walked along the river, they tried to stay under the branches of the dead trees. They walked through brush and over fallen limbs for most of the night. But the farther north they went, the thicker the forest became. Eventually, they could no longer walk under the trees and were forced to walk alongside the riverbank and out in the open. And the riverbank was muddy enough to leave easily tracked footprints.

The woods became thick and impenetrable, and the distance between the water on the left and the wall of twisted dead trees on the right grew narrower. Finally, the trees met the river and they could go no further.

"What do we do now, Toby?" Hoops asked.

"Dewin said follow the river north. This is as far as we can go for now. Let's rest up and try to find a way around in the morning, when we have more light."

In the distance, they heard a crow calling. It was too dark to see anything in the branches of the trees that hung over the river to the south. But it was there, and the sound of the bird was enough to worry the party, especially Eva Mae.

Discovery and Preparation

Braxo watched from the castle walls. The forest was ablaze to the east and the sky was striped just over the treetops as if the morning sun were preparing to rise in the middle of the night. Yet there was no smoke to be seen rising from the distant fire.

The alarm had been raised just a few minutes ago, and Braxo had come out of his chambers ready to pursue the rescue party. When the keeper of the dungeon had awoken from being knocked out, he staggered into the great hall, calling out to whomever would listen, "Help! The prisoner has escaped! Someone alert Lord Braxo!"

Lord Braxo knew they would come for Eva Mae, but he didn't realize it would be so soon after learning about the rescue attempt from his spell. Regardless, when he ended the spell, he made preparations and told his top five dwarven guards to summon all the WolliGuards in the castle.

"How many WolliPogs serve Castle Mavros?" he asked the five.

GurbleWort stepped forward and growled, "One hundred lightly armored with helmet and spear. Another twenty-five with sword and shield. Fifty archers. And twenty-five supply slaves."

"Draw them up in the courtyard. Prepare to march," Braxo calmly ordered.

"Yes, Lord." GurbleWort scurried off with his four comrades following him.

Braxo recalled his conversation with the redheaded boy at Traveler's Rest as he stared off to the fires in the east. *Dewin is with them. He's alive somehow. What is he up to, I wonder? A forest fire to the east while the girl is being sneaked out of my dungeon? That is a clever way to lure the WolliGuard's attention away. GeriPog must have told Dewin to create a forest fire. WolliPogs are terrified of fire... And Dewin would never hurt the forest.*

As the castle guards scrambled to assemble in the courtyard, Braxo walked along the top of the castle walls, scanning the forest to the south, then over to the west. There was nothing but dead forest to the west. All the way to the river, the forest would be thick and difficult to pass through. *I wonder...*

He pulled his dagger from his belt and gave a shrill whistle. The whole castle stopped at the sound and all fell silent except for the *'caw-caw'* of a crow flapping out of Braxo's tower roof. He had left the partition in the dragon-scale roof open after he broke the spell early. One of the crows that nested in the eaves of his chamber answered his whistle and obediently flew down to him through the dark. He stared to the west as the crow landed on his shoulder.

"GurbleWort!" he shouted.

"Yes, Lord."

"Are your troops prepared to march, yet?" Braxo inquired.

"Shortly, my Lord Braxo. We are preparing the supply slaves now," the leader of the castle guard reported from below in the courtyard.

Turning his head to his shoulder, Braxo whispered a command to the crow.

It leapt from his shoulder and flew to the north, to the WolliPog village.

"My Lord, we are assembled and prepared to march," GurbleWort shouted. The guards were lined up in rows of five. Twenty rows of spearmen were in front. Behind them were ten rows of archers. Then came the five rows of swordsmen. The slaves were burdened with food and supplies, ready to follow the small army. At the front stood GurbleWort dressed in a black tunic, emblazoned with a red crescent moon, crossed by a bolt of lightning, the emblem of Braxo and Castle Mavros. He wore a black helmet with horns protruding from each side. There were black leather boots on his feet and in his hands was a double-headed battle axe. His scraggly brown beard was twisted into two braids, and his face had two giant scars that crossed each other, forming an 'X.'

The entire dwarven army had donned their black tunics with the moon and lightning insignia on the chest and back. The leader of each company carried a black flag.

Braxo whistled again. Another crow burst from the tower roof and landed on his shoulder. Again, he whispered a command and sent the dark bird to the west, to search the forest all the way to the river.

He raised his blood-red dagger to the north and closed his eyes. With a quick incantation, he seized control of the crow's mind and eyes. The road was deserted, from the castle, all the way to the village. There was no sign of movement or any sounds from the forest. The crow silently glided over the treetops, searching the forest below along each side of the road. Braxo sent the bird all the way to the burnt remains of the village and found it equally quiet and empty. Releasing the bird's mind, he turned to the west and repeated the spell. With dagger raised and eyes closed, he found the crow and scoured the forest along the river.

When he saw the three children sitting in the dark, he gasped. His excitement was too much for the crow, and it began cawing. *Foolish little winged rat!* He scolded the crow and shut its black beak.

With his army ready to march, he watched the children through the bird's eyes. But they seemed stuck in their path. They were hemmed in with an uncrossable river on their left and a thick wall of brush and trees on their right that choked off any trail to the north.

He knew that Dewin was tricky. The fires to the west were just a distraction to lure the guards away from the dungeon. Dewin was wise enough to know that

Braxo could find the children in the forest eventually. And he suspected that the keeper of the forest would make his move once the army marched out to capture the rescue party.

Braxo had a strategy of his own. "GurbleWort! To the river!"

The dwarf at the head of the WolliPog army nodded. He took a black bull's horn and blew a single low blast. The troops began their march across the drawbridge. When they got to the road that led north, the army veered left and headed west, toward the river. They would have to crawl through a thick forest to get there, but the WolliPog were forest creatures and had no trouble traveling through most terrain. Only the Green Heart was too thick for the WolliPog to penetrate.

Braxo watched as the army, row by row, disappeared into the dead forest to the west. When the last of the supplies slaves vanished into the tree line, he closed his eyes and once again visited the mind of the crow.

Twisted Briar Pass

Dewin stood before his old friend. He had planted Foolinder over forty years ago, and it grew twice as fast as all the others. The old tree wasn't that old, but its roots were strong and deep, and could listen to the silent whispers and moaning of all the other trees in the forest.

"I thought you were dead, Green One," said Foolinder. "The forest has been withering for the past month. And we've been tormented by lightning. Many trees had been lapped up, killed. And Torpil has only been full twice since all of my leaves fell to the ground!"

"I'm pleased to see the lightning hasn't claimed you, my old friend! And with any luck, you'll see Sirihbaz grow green once more." Dewin stood humbly before the wooden face in the tree's trunk. "I greet you with joy... and haste."

"Why the hurry? We have so much to catch up on. Why, just the other day, a traveler passed through here. A *girl*. Can you believe that? A girl traveler! Perhaps things have come full circle."

"The girl is why we have come to you for help. Our friends have rescued her from Braxo's clutches. They are in the forest by the river. At Twisted Briar Pass. Braxo will pursue them, and I need to get to them first. But not too soon," Dewin explained.

"I don't understand. Why endanger the little ones?"

Dewin continued, "I need to make sure Braxo sends his army into the forest towards the river. I can't risk being intercepted on our way to the Green Heart. If Braxo knows we'll be passing through the WolliPog village, he'll beat us there. And all will be lost."

"But if he sends his little trolls into the forest towards the river, you'll be able to get a head start. Is that it?" Foolinder was a clever tree.

Dewin nodded. GeriPog didn't like it when Foolinder referred to the WolliPog as little trolls, but he kept his mouth shut.

Foolinder closed his eyes and let out a grumbly sigh. For a few moments, he was quiet, listening to the trembling and whispers under the ground. The trees talked directly to each other through their roots. The webby network of the forest was still alive, though many of the trees were dying. The old tree could also interpret the language the wind spoke. And trees too distant to talk through their roots would sometimes entrust their words to the wind, to be carried off to the recipient. That was another reason the lightning was so terrifying to the trees. Besides threatening to light them on fire, lightning would electrify the air, zapping the trees' windborne messages, while screaming curses and threats in the trees' ears, if a tree had ears. But the lightning couldn't intercept the underground chatter of trees that lived close to one another.

Foolinder opened his eyes and said, "The forest tells me that the WolliPog army had just entered the forest, heading west."

"Then the time is now. Come, GeriPog," Dewin ordered.

As he walked into the thick forest brush, Foolinder added, "And my river cousins tell me that the children are safe! They have not moved."

"Thank you, Foolinder," Dewin said over his shoulder as he marched due south. "We'll catch up again soon, old friend." As Dewin stepped through the forest, the limbs hanging from the trees around him bent away from him. The brush around his legs scurried aside, leaving a path of clear, soft dirt for his feet. GeriPog followed along as the thick, tangled forest unwound itself and cleared the way for the him and Dewin.

"Wait!" Foolinder tried to shout after them. "Braxo is not with the army... and my name is GrumbleBriar, now!" But it was too late. Dewin moved through Twisted Briar Forest and was already out of earshot.

The forest allowed them to run and run they did. Dewin sprinted ahead, covering vast spans of cleared level ground. GeriPog ran as fast as any dwarf could be expected. Carrying all the gear didn't make it easier. But he never tired as he traveled through Twisted Briar Forest. It was easy to keep going when the forest before you cleared a smooth, flat walkway, and WolliPogs had untiring energy.

The pass ended at a wall of trees that ran right up to a river's edge. The river was on the right, and the wall of tangled trunks and limbs formed a tree line that was so thick, he couldn't see through it. Dewin placed his hand on one of the trees in the wall and whispered some old spell. The trees parted their trunks to either side, making a wide gap for them to pass. But as the gap opened before them like a theater curtain, Toby, Hoops, and Eva Mae stood facing them. They had sprung to their feet when the trees began to move. When Hoops saw Dewin again, he ran over to him and hugged him. It was a relief to see that all was going according to plan.

"GeriPog!" Eva Mae recognized the scarred face of the WolliPog who saved her life. GeriPog stood there looking down at his feet. He felt ashamed. Even though he had saved her life, he had still delivered her to Braxo. No words came. He felt too terrible about himself to even apologize, but as he quickly looked her over for any harm that may have befallen her, he was relieved to see she was unscarred, whole, and freed from the black wizard.

Eva Mae walked over to him, reached down and slipped her little hand into his without saying anything. She stood beside GeriPog as he sobbed.

Green Dewin allowed a few minutes for the party to gather its gear and prepare for the journey ahead. The tears of joy and remorse flowed down GeriPog's face as Eva Mae, his little friend, tenderly wiped them from the scars on his face.

"It's time to go," Dewin ordered. "We must fly quickly through the pass. With any luck, we'll be at the village before noon.

"I hope Aiden made it back!" Hoops said to the group. Aiden had been sent into the forest to the west of the castle. He had done a terrific job setting the beacon fires that distracted the castle guard. He went on his errand alone so that he wouldn't be burdened with having to drag along a slower comrade. Aiden was swift as the wind when he ran. And he needed to use all of his speed to get back to the village on time. They were to meet up at the village at noon, and Aiden had the greatest distance to travel.

Toby reassured the group, "Aiden will be fine. Braxo's WolliGuard army moves slower than a one-legged goat."

The rescue party set off to the north, through Twisted Briar Pass. The gap in the trees closed behind them, blocking off any who might try to follow, and the path before them graciously cleared itself as they ran through the wood.

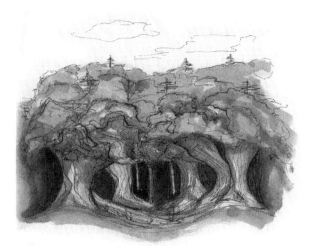

Race to The Village

Braxo's eyes were closed, and his hand stretched out towards the river. He had control of the crow's mind still and had landed it in the branches of the trees across the river. It took great effort to keep the black bird silent as it watched the three travelers rendezvous with his old enemy. When he saw GeriPog holding the girl's hand, his anger burned like a cauldron. He looked forward to his next opportunity to punish the dwarf for his betrayal.

As the rescue party disappeared into the thick forest to the north, Braxo commanded the crow to return. He scribbled a note on some parchment, tied it to the crow's foot, and sent him back into the forest to seek out GurbleWort and the army. They had not gotten halfway through the forest towards the river when the bird reached them.

GurbleWort untied the note and read Braxo's order: "Return to the castle and take the road north to the village as fast as you can."

"HALT!" the dwarf general shouted to the army of two hundred WolliPogs. "Back to the castle at once! GO!" The entire army did an about face and tramped back through the woods the way they had come. Every one of them grumbled and complained. GurbleWort complained louder than any of them.

Braxo stood at the foot of the drawbridge as the army emerged from the woods, his crow resting on his right shoulder. When the army came to a stop on the road in front of the castle, Braxo pulled from his pocket a small chunk of purple crystal. He held it close to his lips as he chanted an incantation. He offered it to the crow, who grabbed it with his beak and quickly swallowed it. Braxo pointed to the army and the crow took to the air, flying in circles above the heads of the two hundred mean little dwarves. As the crow flapped its wings, the entire bird evaporated into a black smoke. This smoke thickened into an opaque, black cloud that hovered for a few minutes just feet above the army.

"We will march north to the village," Braxo hissed as the cloud lowered itself into the midst of the WolliPogs. "We will run swiftly and quietly. No one is allowed to speak. We will wait unseen and capture them there."

The entire army was cloaked by the spell. Each dwarf became invisible except for the footprints they left in the road's dirt. Braxo was the last to disappear as he led them towards the village. As they marched up the road, only the sound of their boots and the clanging of their armor could be heard.

*****

The journey through Twisted Briar Pass ended when Dewin and the brave travelers reached Foolinder, the old tree.

"You've made it back safely, I see," the old tree said to the group. "Did you find any trouble along the way?

Dewin answered, "We moved quickly and found no trouble, Foolinder."

"His name is *Foolinder?*" Eva Mae asked Dewin giggling. "I met him before anyone else when I arrived in the world, and we talked for a long time."

"Indeed we did, little friend," the tree interjected. "And you gave me a wonderful new name. I've been working hard to make sure all my cousins know it. *GrumbleBriar!*"

"Oh?" said Dewin, "GrumbleBriar, is it? Well then, GrumbleBriar, can you tell me where Braxo and his army were last seen? I'd like to avoid any entanglements getting these young ones back to safety."

GrumbleBriar closed his eyes and reached out to all the trees of the forest that he could reach with his roots.

"There is confusion, Dewin," he said with his eyes shut. "The forest can't find them. The trees don't see them anywhere. The wind carries sounds of footsteps and armor. And of course the smell of WolliFart."

GeriPog didn't like it when the old tree talked about the WolliPog that way. "Does it carry the smell of woodsmoke, too? I love the smell of burning deadwood." It was a threat. GeriPog never cared for the talking tree and would gladly take his axe to it.

GrumbleBriar pretended to ignore the threat at first, but then replied, "It does, actually. I know you lit those poor trees on fire in the eastern wood, you little WolliTurd. How is it that you're so adept at killing things with those little sausage fingers, hmmm?"

"How is it that a tree with a mouth as big as yours has avoided an axe all these years?" GeriPog was getting angry. He bounced his axe in his hands and was ready to separate GrumbleBriar's face from his trunk.

"Well, I think we'll be on our way, old friend." Green Dewin jumped between GeriPog and the old tree. The three children just watched as the tree and the dwarf argued. Dewin had been hoping for a better report of Braxo's army, but the tree didn't seem all that cooperative anymore, thanks to the dwarf.

"Farewell. Don't forget to come back and visit 'ol GrumbleBriar sometime. I'm not going anywhere." He laughed as the party headed west towards the village.

They walked quickly through light forests of leafless trees. But they weren't dying anymore. Just a week ago, they were dead as dead could be. Now, they were starting to bud. The tiny green pods at the tips of every branch and twig promised a return of life.

When Eva Mae asked GeriPog about the buds, the old dwarf replied, "It's because Green Dewin has returned from the dead. He's the spirit of the forest, you know."

Over low hills and through shady glens, they traveled. Eva Mae remembered the landscape well. But when she had come this way a week ago, the sky crackled with lightning. Several trees had

suspicion: he might not need the timepiece at all to escape Sirihbaz! And when this 'rescue party' headed back to Traveler's Rest, he would follow them to discover how they do it.

"Well?" Hoops addressed the group. "Should we get going? I'm not feeling safe just standing here out in the open."

Eva Mae agreed, "Yeah. Let's get back into the forest. Something doesn't feel right here."

"What do you mean, Eva Mae?" Dewin asked.

"It doesn't feel safe. It feels... it's just... Oh, I don't know how to say it. It feels dark-like and sad. The way things felt in that castle when Braxo was showing off his magic." She hung her head and shivered as she remembered the bony, invisible hands that would slap and grab her.

"You'll have to tell me all about the magic you saw, Eva Mae. When we return to Traveler's Rest to get your timepiece, you and I will sit and talk all about the things you experienced in Castle Mavros. There is much to be learned," Dewin spoke gently, but the urgency in his voice was all the group needed to hear.

They headed east to the other side of the village, walking in single file with Toby in the very back. Braxo, invisible from his spell, slithered behind them at a distance of ten yards as they walked across the field to the forest's edge. Once they were inside the forest, Braxo followed further back, perhaps fifty or more yards. Just because he was invisible, didn't mean they couldn't hear a stick break or shrubs rustling as he stalked them.

The party continued walking due east. They hiked as fast as they could as a group and had traveled a full mile into the forest before coming to the base of a hill. Eva Mae instantly recognized where they were.

"Nose rock is just on the other side of this hill!" she shouted.

GeriPog confirmed her observation. "It is, girl. You have an excellent sense of direction. But we'll not have time for any fire. We're not stopping at the nose."

Braxo slid closer to eavesdrop.

"Where are we going, then?" asked Eva Mae.

Hoops jumped in, "The portal."

Eva Mae was confused so Dewin took a second to explain, "Sirihbaz has an ancient doorway. It's connected to the other worlds by what is known as the 'Chamber of Crossroads,' the great junction of all twelve worlds of the timepiece. Sirihbaz's portal that leads directly to the chamber is hidden nearby."

"So there is a portal in every world?" Eva Mae asked.

"Indeed, there is, little one," said Dewin.

"So if Braxo finds out, it'll be over. He won't need the timepiece anymore. He'll be able to travel freely to all the worlds, *including* Traveler's Rest. We wouldn't stand a chance against him," Toby explained. "We have to get out of Sirihbaz as fast as we can. He's on his way to the village with his army. I just know it. And If he sees where the portal is hidden, we'll be in big trouble."

Too late. Braxo smiled to himself. His suspicions had been confirmed and he brimmed with excitement to find this portal. *And a chamber that connected all the worlds?* It sounded like the perfect place to establish his new throne.

The group scurried up the hill to its sparsely wooded top. Only Eva Mae and Hoops turned around to take in the landscape of Sirihbaz's forests and the little WolliPog village. Somewhere back down the hill, Eva Mae thought she heard something. Maybe a stick broke. Maybe it was just a squirrel or something. She wasn't sure, and it had stopped moving, whatever it was. She said nothing and grabbed Hoops by the hand. They both ran to catch up to the group.

Braxo was more careful coming down the other side of the hill than he was going up. He almost blew his cover when he stepped on some dead branches. But this time, he took care to move slowly, gliding from tree to tree, staying as far back as he could without losing sight of his enemies.

He followed them to the bottom of the hill, right up to the wall of the Green Heart. It was a nasty tangle of dead trees so thick, they were impassible. It was like a swamp of forest trees, surrounded by a ring of hills. Nothing could live here, it was a useless tumor of forest that had to be avoided when traveling between the WolliPog village and Castle Mavros. Braxo had tried many times before to burn out the Green Heart with lightning, but it wouldn't catch. Probably it was too soggy and boggy to catch fire.

The rescue party had turned left and walked along the wall of trees rounding the Green Heart to the north. Eventually, the hills that rose above them on the left were replaced by rock formations and cliffs. The rocky cliffs eventually ran right up to the Green Heart's wall of tangled trees on the right. This was the end of the trail. This was the 'pinch,' where Braxo and GeriPog had corralled and captured a bunch of WolliPog slaves long ago.

Braxo followed at about thirty yards behind, when the party stopped at the 'pinch.' And one by one, they slipped into some hidden opening in the Green Heart's wooden wall. When Toby, who was at the back of the group, slipped through the hole, Braxo had managed to get close enough to see.

The passage was barely big enough for Braxo to crawl into and was certainly big enough for an army of WolliPogs to pass through, if they walked single file.

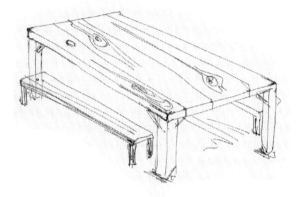

Traveler's Un-Rest

"What happened to your face?!" Toby gasped.

Eli's eyes were black and blue with a bandage across his nose. His nostrils were dirty from dried blood. He was a tough kid, but the assault he endured had left him weaker than normal and disheartened. Still, he had his checklists and journals in his arms as he made his rounds. He was a dedicated Keeper, perhaps the best that the Traveler's League had ever voted into office.

Eli kept his eyes on his journals and sniffed. "Smitty." He didn't say anything else. His feelings were hurt and he wasn't in a talking mood. The rest of the boys in Traveler's Rest burst with excitement when Dewin, Toby, Aiden, and Hoops arrived with GeriPog and the mysterious girl. Eli stayed back, embarrassed by his appearance and the throttling he had received from the captain.

Many of the boys were still unsure about a girl being selected to travel with the timepiece. The Old Rule had been broken, thanks to Hoops, and they would all have to decide whether she would be worthy of joining the league. That wouldn't happen, of course, if she didn't get to finish her travels with the timepiece. In the meantime, many boys sat at a long table across from Eva Mae and GeriPog. They fired question after question about Sirihbaz, Castle Mavros, and Braxo. Eva Mae loved having the company of more kids her age, and didn't care that they were all boys. And when a boy would say something rude about pigtails or dresses or the inferiority of girls, GeriPog would slam his chubby fist down on the table or quickly stand to his feet and grimace at them. It was enough to keep the boys from being too disrespectful, as boys sometimes could be. Eva Mae felt protected when she was with GeriPog, and as a matter of fact, even though she was surrounded by kids her own age who were brave and good, and even though she was in the company of a kind and gentle wizard, she chose to stay close to the dwarf. GeriPog was her best friend in the world, in all of the worlds. Hoops was a little jealous of their friendship, often wondering what had happened to old WolliTom. He feared the worst, that WolliTom might be dead, and was afraid to ask GeriPog. So, he kept quiet and hoped that one day he would see WolliTom again.

Dewin and Toby pleaded with Eli to sit alone with them and talk about what had happened. Eli eventually relented and the three of them huddled at a table in a quiet corner on the other side of the clubhouse.

"After you left," Eli began, "Smitty was really moody. He came over here and sat at this same table and just... well, pouted."

"He's probably embarrassed. I should've handled things better," said Toby.

"Nonsense, Toby. You showed great leadership and calm," Dewin reassured him. "Besides, if not for you, GeriPog could've been killed. And who knows what

Smitty would have done to Hoops if he had gotten too carried away." Dewin stared at the table as he talked. "I fear he may let his bitterness grow too deep. He is a stubborn and hot-headed boy."

Toby turned to Eli. "Where is Smitty, anyway??"

"He used the timepiece after he..." Eli was too embarrassed to tell them the details about his broken nose. "I don't think anybody saw what time he set it too."

Toby grew angrier, imagining Smitty punching Eli and acting like a jerk. "Why did he hit you, Eli? Did you say something to make him angry? I mean, what the heck happened?"

"I was taking inventory, like always. Then I blacked out. The next thing I know, Smitty is on top of me. Hitting me in the face." Eli was silent for a few seconds, took a deep breath, and then confessed, "The other boys heard Smitty yell, 'BRAXO' as he jumped on me. I don't remember that, though." Eli was wracked with shame. He felt that Braxo had taken something from him. "I can't believe that Braxo took control of me. I'm so sorry."

"Stop that ridiculous nonsense!" Dewin barked. Eli sat straight up and stared wide eyed at the wizard. "It wasn't your fault, Eli. There's not a boy here who blames you for anything. Braxo could have seized any of these boys' minds."

"Dewin's right, Eli." Toby put his hand on the Keeper's shoulder. "You were just unlucky. Braxo is to blame... and Smitty." His eyes darkened with anger. The violation of leadership and the bully behavior of the redheaded captain couldn't go unpunished.

The two boys and the wizard sat quietly for a while. They watched the brave boys of the Traveler's League surround Eva Mae, sharing stories about all their adventures. Eva Mae sat like a little queen, straight and tall, with GeriPog, her guardian, at her side. She had a special presence that made her the most interesting person to ever visit Traveler's Rest. If Smitty were there and called for the boys to vote on Eva Mae's membership in the league, it seemed they might actually permit it.

Dewin broke the silence at his table. "She's not done, you know. She needs to finish her travels with the timepiece."

"But Smitty has it," Eli said.

"Yeah, good luck prying it from his greedy fingers. The *jerk*." Toby had a cool, deep anger firmly set against Smitty. It would only be a matter of time before he confronted the captain and demanded that the league vote to replace him with someone else. Toby was willing to serve as captain, but if the league thought a different boy should do it, so be it; anybody but Smitty. He had gone too far.

Dewin slowly rose to his feet. "Eli, we will need provisions. I'm afraid our rescue party is not quite ready to disband. We must scour the Four Gates and Five Worlds until we catch Smitty and take back the timepiece." He looked at Toby and raised his bushy eyebrow. "What do you say, Retriever?"

"I'm in," Toby said from behind the black hair swooping over half his face. He was ready to take the timepiece back *and* take off Smitty's snotty red head. "Who else should we pick to go with us?"

Dewin looked across the room. In the crowd of boys surrounding Eva Mae, many brave travelers would be a good companion for this new journey. Only a few may not be up to the task. But Dewin had no doubt that if he asked them, all of them would volunteer. "We should ask the travelers. I'm not the captain, Toby. And neither are you. These boys can't be ordered. We can only ask for volunteers."

The wizard strode across the clubhouse and cleared his throat. When he did, the boys quit their chatting. As they turned their attention to Dewin, he told them of the new quest he and Toby would undertake. They all listened quietly. When Dewin had finished speaking, Toby asked the boys who would like to volunteer to join him. It didn't surprise Dewin that every single boy raised his hand.

Toby asked that a second group of volunteers be formed to stay at Traveler's Rest to guard Eli and Eva Mae, and possibly catch Smitty if he showed the nerve to come back. Again, every single hand went up.

"You can't do both." Toby laughed. "Some will have to go and some have to stay... and I can't decide for you. I'm not your captain."

"You should be," Aiden raised his voice from behind the crowd.

The gang of travelers all seemed to agree. Another boy named Christian poked his blond head out from behind Hoops, who stood at the front of the group. "Maybe we should vote on it, guys."

Eli stepped forward and told the boys that a simple majority vote wouldn't count. Majority votes were good enough to decide whether someone could be a member of the league. But a vote for who should be captain had to be unanimous.

Aiden spoke up again, "I nominate Toby to be our captain. All in favor?"

Every hand went up except Toby's. It was against the rules to vote for yourself. And Toby wouldn't have voted for himself anyway.

"It's settled. Toby is the new captain of the Traveler's League." Eli smiled while the boys cheered. They all crowded in and shook the hand of their new leader. When they were done, Toby spoke up.

"I'd like Hoops, Aiden, and GeriPog to join us on the mission. Christian?"

"Yes, Cap."

"I need you to stay here and be head of the guard while we're away. Keep the boys armed and ready to snare Smitty. Eli will keep you provisioned. You're in charge while I'm away."

"Understood, Cap." Christian selected boys to make up his troop of guards. There were about thirty boys willing to stay behind and help Christian. They called themselves "The Club Knights." Eli handed out swords, round, wooden shields, spears, helmets... and nets.

The rest of the boys were ready to search for Smitty. Twenty-five in all. And since Christian had given his group a cool nickname, the group going off with Toby decided to call themselves "The Fox Hunters." Many of the boys had already referred to Smitty as 'the fox' due to his red hair and preference to always be alone. He was smart like a fox as well, but the name wasn't a compliment. The Fox Hunters were the faster and more experienced boys, many of them having visited each world more than just once. None of them would have any issues confronting Smitty when they found him. Smitty had lost all loyalty.

Since Christian was chosen to lead the Club Knights, Toby asked Aiden to be the leader of the Fox Hunters as his second in command. Hoops was too new to be put in charge of the group.

Dewin, GeriPog, and Toby rallied the Fox Hunters together and Eli ran all over the clubhouse getting supplies packed up. He handed out backpacks containing food, first aid, fresh socks, matches, and a journal and pen. Along with the backpacks, he handed out a different weapon to each Fox Hunter. Many of the boys would examine their weapon and trade with another boy. After about thirty minutes of preparation, the Hunters were ready to leave.

Dewin, GeriPog, and Toby led the group, single file, through the portal that led to the Chamber of Crossroads. Christian pulled back the big yellow curtain and stood by the portal. He and his Knights wished each traveler 'good luck' as they disappeared, one by one, into the glowing disk embedded in the wall of the clubhouse. Hoops was the last to go through, and just before he did, he slipped the hood of his magic cloak over his head.

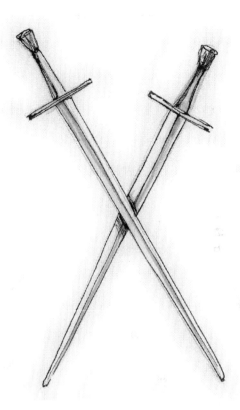

Surprise, Surprise

"Welcome, Green One!" Braxo's voice boomed. When Dewin, GeriPog, and Toby emerged from the portal into the chamber, they were greeted by the sight of two hundred armed WolliGuards who immediately surrounded them. Before Dewin could raise his hands or summon any magic, Braxo had reached out and seized him with his invisible, bony hands.

As each Hunter stepped through the portal from Traveler's Rest into the chamber, they were surrounded by the dwarven army and corralled to the center of the chamber. Braxo had discovered the portal in Sirihbaz but went back for his army before entering. He knew he would eventually capture his enemies if he waited. And now that he was free to roam the worlds without the timepiece, he decided to use the chamber as his throne room.

The black portal in the top of the domed chamber swirled violently. It was a storm of black smoke, twisting and churning with excitement.

"You foolish boy!" Dewin yelled at Braxo. "You're going to get us all killed."

Braxo snapped back, "Silence!" An invisible force struck Dewin across the face.

When the twenty-fourth boy stepped through the portal, and into Braxo's trap, he was forced to join his fellow captors at the center of the chamber, directly under a giant, glowing, green crystal hovered about ten feet in the air.

Hoops was the last to step through, but nobody saw him on account of his cloak. The sight of Braxo and the WolliPog army stunned and terrified him, but he kept quiet.

"Drop your weapons," GurbleWort ordered the Fox Hunters. The surrounding army had spears and swords leveled, ready to strike and stab the entire group.

"Do as he says, boys," Dewin relented. The boys dropped their swords, spears, clubs, hatchets, and knives. The clanging of the falling metal filled the chamber with the echo of defeat.

Hoops slipped back into the portal to Traveler's Rest unseen.

Braxo bragged about having escaped Sirihbaz. He went on and on about how he would invade the Five Worlds and rule them all.

"And when I'm done destroying Traveler's Rest, I will take my army, and my unmatched power, and go back home. I will rule Earth." Braxo laughed like only a villain could. "They have no idea what's coming. The power. The terror."

"You're insane, boy," GeriPog shouted. "I should have ended your life forty years ago when I found you in that ravine... crying like a baby."

The swirling in the portal above grew more violent, but Braxo didn't seem to notice.

"How dare you talk to your master like that, you dirty little troll! GurbleWort, teach this traitor some respect," Braxo hissed.

The new general of the WolliGuard gripped his axe in both hands and walked towards the group of surrendered travelers. The armed dwarfs stepped aside, making a path for their leader with the horned helmet. When GurbleWort finally stood toe to toe with GeriPog, he shoved the handle of the axe into his stomach, knocking the wind out of him. GurbleWort punched at GeriPog's scarred face and he fell to his knees. Dewin struggled to free himself from Braxo's magic invisible grip but he couldn't even turn his head.

"You devil!" Dewin yelled at GurbleWort. "Striking your own kind, like some rabid dog. He's your kin. YOU are the only traitor in this room."

Braxo ordered a gag to be put in Dewin's mouth. A handful of WolliGuards set to work silencing the green wizard. When they were done, Braxo waved his hand and Dewin was spun to his left, facing GeriPog and GurbleWort.

"Now you can see your friend," Braxo said, "and watch him die for his insolence." The black wizard nodded his head toward GurbleWort, who then lifted his great, double-headed axe above his head.

"CLUB KNIGHTS, ATTACK!" The yell echoed through the chamber, startling everyone, good and wicked alike. Christian dashed through the portal from Traveler's Rest with a longsword held out before him in one hand, and a round, wooden shield in the other. Other boys with spears, sword, and hatchets raced into the chamber behind him. The shocked WolliGuards near the portal hadn't even turned around before they fell dead. Boy after boy entered the chamber armed to the teeth and wild for a fight. The WolliGuard army tried to form itself into some kind of disciplined line, but the wild boys were all around the chamber, coming at them from every angle.

GurbleWort had been startled and forgot to bring his axe down on GeriPog. He ran after the armed Club Knights entering the chamber. The chaos from the attack was enough for Braxo to lose his concentration and Dewin was released from his magic grip. The Hunters, clustered in the center of the chamber, picked up their weapons and fought off the black-clothed dwarves that surrounded them.

The sound of metal crashing against metal was deafening. Boys and dwarves shouted insults at each other as they slashed and stabbed.

Braxo slithered through the chamber towards Christian, but Dewin stepped between them. His arms raised, he muttered an ancient spell and reached his hands out towards the black wizard. His hands turned into brown limbs that stretched out and crawled through the air. When his wooden fingertips reached Braxo, they wound around him like living vines. Before Braxo was completely covered with the crawling, weedy tentacles, he managed to get one arm free and pull out his black dagger. He slashed the two main vines that led straight to Dewin's arms, cutting them off completely. His wavy, red blade sliced through the green wood like a hot knife sliding through a stick of butter. Dewin screamed in pain and the vines that wrapped around Braxo broke free, fell to the ground, and vanished. Dewin's wooden arms retracted and his normal hands and fingers returned.

Braxo stretched his arm out to his right side and used his invisible, bony hands to grab a nearby traveler. He lifted the boy into the air and tossed him at the green wizard. The boy flew through the air, arms and legs flailing as he hurled towards Dewin. But the Old Green One put his palms together and shouted, "Foolinder!" disappearing in an explosion of autumn leaves that fell to the stone floor in a big pile. The pile of red and gold leaves cushioned the flying boy when he landed butt-first, unharmed. Braxo didn't see Dewin reappear behind him. The green wizard inhaled, filling his lungs with as big of a breath as he could, then closed his eyes. The sound of it caused Braxo to turn around, just as Dewin released his breath and blew an icy wind, mixed with snow and sleet right in Braxo's face. Braxo yelled in pain as he stumbled backwards, covering his frostbitten cheeks with the left sleeve of his black cloak. He tripped over the boy he had thrown across the room only moments before, and he fell backwards into the leaves and onto his back. He tried to get up but only made it onto his knees as he continued to cover his face. The icy wind was so vicious, forceful, and cold that he couldn't stand at all. Within a few seconds, Braxo's kneeling body had been encased in a giant chunk of ice.

Dewin called for Toby, but the captain was locked in battle with GurbleWort and three other WolliGuards. Toby's skill with the sword was unmatched and his footwork was like a dancer. Still, it was obvious the he was tiring. Across the room, Aiden eluded a dozen or so dwarves with his unbelievable quickness. One WolliGuard thrust at him with a spear, but Aiden moved so quickly, by the time the dwarf pulled his spear back, Aiden's wooden staff already struck the scarred face of the dwarf.

With Braxo temporarily stuck in the ice block, Dewin had time to move across the chamber and help the injured. There were a dozen boys who had been cut, stabbed, and knocked down. Some were bleeding and crying, and others were unconscious, lying on the ground as if dead. But Green Dewin would heal them. One of the Hunters had a terrible gash in his right forearm. Dewin lifted the boy's arm and breathed on the wound. The icy breath soothed the pain and stopped the bleeding immediately. Then Dewin placed his hand over the cut for a few moments. When he pulled his hand back, a bandage of herbs and leaves was wrapped snugly around the boy's forearm. With the pain gone, the boy jumped to his feet, grabbed his hatchet and rejoined the fight.

Hoops had removed the hood of his cloak when Dewin froze Braxo. He ran to the wizard's side to fight off any enemies while Dewin tended to the tired, injured travelers.

The problem arose that the boys, both Fox Hunters and Club Knights, were getting tired. WolliPogs had inexhaustible energy, even if they were a little slow. Still living, he would keep fighting and fighting without ever worrying his strength might die out. The boys were getting struck down faster than Dewin could heal them and restore their strength.

"We're losing this fight, Hoops" Dewin said with a solemn face. "We need to turn the tide quickly, or we'll be forced to retreat into one of the five worlds. The ice will melt eventually. Braxo won't be stuck much longer."

Hoops' mind raced as he watched the WolliGuards fight back against the tiring boys. *There must be a way to fight off this army of dwarves. They won't get tired. We need something stronger than them to fight back.*

An idea so crazy, so unbelievably insane, flashed across his mind. *It HAS to work, though. I have to do it.*

"I'll be right back, Dewin." Hoops took off across the chamber towards one of the portals.

"Wait, Hoops! Where are you going? We need you here, boy!" Dewin was unsure of what the golden-headed ten-year-old had planned, but the travelers needed every fighter they could keep on their feet at that moment.

"You'll see! I won't be long," Hoops yelled back over his shoulder just before disappearing through a portal. On the floor below the glowing disc, etched in the stone was the Roman numeral for 'one.'

The Rampage

The fight wasn't going well. There were still at least sixty dwarves on their feet fighting against the Traveler's League. Still outnumbered, the boys fought ferociously with every ounce of strength they had left. Dewin felt proud to see these young men fight for one another so bravely. He was also sad thinking that this could be the end of them altogether. He couldn't use his magic to fight while he was busy healing the boys who needed him. There just wasn't enough time, and the boys were starting to lose.

The WolliGuard army had formed a semicircle around the group of travelers, backing them up against the wall of the chamber. They tried to drive the boys out of the chamber through the portals.

"Do not retreat, boys. We must hold our ground and not surrender the chamber to Braxo!" Dewin yelled as he tended to a boy with a broken leg.

GeriPog fought between Toby and Aiden. On the other side of Toby, Christian thrashed at the WolliGuards with his blade, like a wild animal. Only about twenty travelers were on their feet fighting back. It was three to one and the odds were getting worse by the second.

GurbleWort suddenly ordered the dwarves to stop fighting and fall back to him. The boys stood panting, exhausted and half-crazed with the shock of battle. Braxo's dwarf general ordered the WolliGuards to form a line that stretched across the chamber. They had the swordsmen in the front row lock their shields together, forming a wall. The spearmen of the second row extended the points of their spears over the shield wall. The rest of the army stood behind them, ready to continue the fight.

"Advance!" ordered GurbleWort. The army stepped together and slowly marched toward the huddled group of travelers.

"We've lost, Dewin. We have to get out of here," cried Toby.

But before Dewin could respond, Christian yelled out, "What's that?"

A loud, bellowing roar filled the chamber, echoing off the walls. It was so loud, half of the WolliGuards dropped their weapons to cover their ears. There was a great commotion somewhere behind the wall of shields and dwarves in the back ranks screamed out in terror. But the travelers couldn't see what was happening.

ROARRRRRRRR! The thundering bellow of a monster again rang through the chamber.

After several more screams, the WolliGuard shield wall broke apart and dwarves ran in every direction in a panic. A great beast with vicious black horns charged through the chamber, goring dwarf after dwarf. The beast was as large as an elephant and had leathery orange skin. It had a long neck like a horse and the jaws of a crocodile. It had dark-brown hair on its shoulders running down the ridge of its back, as well as hair on its chin that ran down its neck to its chest. Along with the two great horns curving forward from its head, it also had a horn like a rhino at the tip of its wicked snout. There were three black claws on each of its feet.

The monster sprang across the chamber and skewered two WolliGuards at once. With a swing of its head, the dwarves slid off its horns and fell to the ground, dead. Its next victim was a spearman who wasn't fast enough. He ended his life between the jaws of the ridgeback toxigator.

Hoops was in control of the beast's mind. He stood somewhere in the jungle of Isango, directing every movement of the toxigator.

The WolliGuard army was beside itself with fright. The guards that were too scared to run, were gobbled up, crushed, mauled, and trampled. The rest ran around like crazy... until the monster caught them. By the time it was over, only a dozen WolliGuards remained. In a panic, they jumped into whatever portal was nearest them to escape certain death.

The Traveler's League cheered the beast as it did its bloody work. When there were no more WolliGuards to devour, the beast slowly walked over to Green Dewin and lowered its head in a dramatic bow. Hoops took a bow for a brilliant performance through the mind of the toxigator. When the monster raised its head, it gave one last triumphant roar, before galloping back into the portal from which it had emerged.

Hoops returned to the chamber a few minutes later. He was in his own body again and arrived as Dewin, Toby, GeriPog, and Aiden helped Christian and his remaining Knights carry the wounded boys back into Traveler's Rest. One by one, the boys were helped off the floor and assisted by their brothers. The chamber finally was empty except for Dewin, GeriPog, and Hoops.

"What will we do about *that?*" GeriPog pointed his fat little finger at the block of ice encasing Braxo. Water puddled on the stone floor as the ice melted.

"I'll stay here to deal with Braxo. Hoops... you must go back and tend to the travelers. After I've taken care of Braxo, we can find Smitty and retrieve the timepiece." Dewin turned to GeriPog. "I need you to watch over the girl until we get the timepiece back. She is in your care, GeriPog. You must keep her safe."

GeriPog simply bowed and headed back through the portal to Traveler's Rest. But Hoops didn't want to leave Dewin alone with Braxo. Braxo was as deadly and dangerous as he was tricky. Dewin saw that his friend had no intention of leaving quite yet, and though he didn't want him to see the dark work he must perform, he knew that ordering a boy like Hoops to go away was pointless. He would pretend to obey, then put his cloak on and come back and watch you from the safety of invisibility.

"You've made good use of the gifts that WolliTom and I gave you. Do you still have your dagger on you, Hoops?"

Hoops slipped it from its sheath and held it out for Dewin to see. "Yes, sir."

"Good." Dewin sighed. "I need you to fetch the girl now."

Hoops slipped into Traveler's Rest. Eva Mae sat with GeriPog, listening to Christian retell the details of the great battle with the WolliGuard army. Hoops interrupted and asked Eva Mae to follow him.

"Dewin needs your help with something. He told me to get you."

Eva Mae got up, and GeriPog followed.

"Dewin didn't ask for you, GeriPog," Hoops ordered. "I think he wanted you to stay here."

"He told me to protect the girl, boy. How do you expect me to do that from a world away?" the dwarf grumbled. "I'm going. Don't bother trying to stop me." GeriPog pushed his way past Hoops and took Eva Mae's hand. With Hoops behind them, they slipped through the glowing

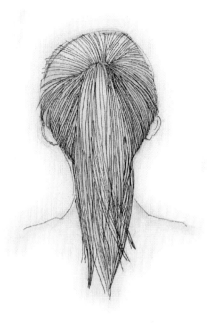

Prophecy Fulfilled

The chamber was heavy with warm, balmy air. Thickening black clouds rolled across the domed ceiling, flickering with lightning. A dense fog filled the chamber and only a faint, green glow could be seen towards the middle. Thunder peeled, and the room grew darker. Somewhere in the fog, Dewin cried out in pain.

Hoops, Eva Mae, and GeriPog listened in horror. Another scream from

Dewin echoed through the fog. They couldn't tell from where.

"We need to find him. Something's wrong." GeriPog sniffed the air like a dog. Another flash of lightning brought more thunder and somewhere in the center of the chamber, they heard Braxo laughing. Then Dewin screamed again.

"He's escaped!" GeriPog gasped.

"Dewin! Where are you?" Hoops yelled. He headed into the fog, but GeriPog grabbed his arm.

"NO, boy. It's too dangerous. Look!" GeriPog pointed to the ceiling. Four, long, black tentacles of smoke stretched out from the portal in the center of the ceiling. They reached into the fog below, searching for anything they could find. The black storm clouds around the portal churned counterclockwise about the chamber. The moans and screams from the unlucky souls trapped within the black portal grew louder. Hoops could hear them between the rolls of thunder.

"You can't let those things get a hold of you. We should stay together. We'll move along the wall and search for Dewin." GeriPog tried to act like he wasn't afraid, but Hoops noticed the slight tremor in the dwarf's hands as he pulled him alongside the wall.

"When we find him," Hoops said as they cautiously walked, "I'll use my cloak to go for help." He gripped the handle of his knife.

Dewin screamed again. It was getting worse.

"Stay close to me, girl. And be brave..." GeriPog turned to grab Eva Mae's hand, but she was gone.

*****

The air smelled like sulfur. It reminded Eva Mae of burnt-out fireworks and the nasty sewer of Castle Mavros. It was hard not to gag thinking about it. She strained to hear Dewin, but his screams softened, and the moaning and screaming from the portal above grew louder. She couldn't tell which direction Dewin's screams might be coming from. Step after step took her closer to the only thing visible in the fog... the soft, green light in the middle of the chamber. But it was getting softer. She wasn't sure if the green crystal was darkening or if the clouds and fog were thickening. Finally, she arrived at the middle of the chamber. There was no fog in the center of the room. In fact, it was a bubble, or pocket of air, cocooned by the storm clouds above and the fog all around. There, directly underneath the hovering crystal lay Dewin's body, half-formed into a tree. His legs were gone, replaced by a twisted tree trunk. Its roots dug into the stone floor. Braxo's magic pulled at his chest and arms. Limbs and branches popped out of his body like spears thrusting from the inside out. With every new branch that shot out from his chest or back, the green wizard screamed in pain. Standing before him was Braxo, laughing hysterically. He had broken off a piece of the green crystal somehow and held it out before him, towards Dewin. In his other hand was his blood-red dagger.

Eva Mae watched in horror as Braxo finished his work. The Old Green One had been completely transformed into a tree. All that remained was the face of the kind wizard, firmly embedded in the tree's trunk. The branches and limbs stretched outward and upward in a way that twisted around the base of the green crystal. Dewin's new wooden tree form now held the crystal aloft in the air, but no leaves grew in his branches.

Braxo's back was turned to Eva Mae, and when Dewin's transformation was complete, Braxo walked right up to his now wooden face.

"It's over, Dewin. You are mine. The chamber is mine. The girl is mine," he hissed as he carved into the wood with his dagger. Dewin screamed, but his voice was low and scratchy, just like GrumbleBriar's. "The boy is mine. The travelers are mine. The timepiece is MINE," Dewin screamed again as Braxo finished carving the crescent and lightning bolt into the wood above his face.

The sadness and anger in the little girl's heart was unbearable. She cried as she watched her friend be tortured. Braxo couldn't hear her from all the screaming and thundering. Tears trickled down her cheeks as she reached into her pocket. Her fingers found the small chunk of dark-purple crystal and she wrapped her fist around it. She thrust out her other hand and imagined that Braxo was the wooden chair from the castle. She imagined his body was made from old, rotted-out wood. She imagined his arms and legs to be wobbly, old chair legs. She could feel the weakness in the frame of his body and as the crystal glowed in her fist, she squeezed her outstretched hand, closing her fingers.

Braxo's laugh was cut off. He dropped both his dagger and the green crystal at the same time. With both hands, he grabbed at his neck, trying to pry away the invisible, bony fingers crushing his throat. Eva Mae lifted her arm and Braxo rose into the air. His legs kicked and dangled as he struggled for breath. With another squeeze of her fist, his eyeballs opened wide and his face turned purple. She raised her arm higher and pointed it at the swirling disc in the ceiling above. Braxo rose higher into the chamber. The four black tentacles found him and wrapped themselves around his face and neck. Eva Mae could feel them tugging at Braxo's body, but she didn't tug back. She raised him higher, and all at once, the tentacles yanked Braxo free from her magical, unseen grip and drew him into the black, swirling portal.

Braxo's screaming was unbearable and sickening. Lightning flashed all around and the thunder boomed over and over. But both lightning and thunder diminished as Braxo's screams became softer and softer as he was sucked farther and farther into the blackness of the shadow wizard's realm of death. When his final scream went out, the clouds and fog in the chamber vanished, and the green crystal again lit the room with its warm glow.

Eva Mae ran to the tree that held the crystal above the floor. She wrapped her arms around the Old Green One and cried, "I'm so sorry, Dewin."

A scratchy and weak old voice, wracked with pain, eked out of the face in the tree trunk, "Youuuu... d... d... did... w... well, little one."

Hoops and GeriPog rushed to Eva Mae. Their eyes were wide with astonishment and their mouths gaped as they beheld the leafless tree that was once the green wizard. They couldn't find any words to comfort their old friend, or the little girl crying before the tree's twisted trunk.

"F... f... find... th... the... timepiece," Dewin told them before closing his wooden eyelids and slipping into a deep winter's sleep.

The End

Note from the Author

NICHOLAS GOSS has been a piano teacher, sailboat builder, private investigator, barista, and salesman. He has a collection of more books than he could possible read in his lifetime and lives with his head firmly stuck in the clouds. He resides in Nashville with his wife, two kids, and their labradoodle, Shelby. His host of eccentric hobbies include woodworking, sailing, fencing, ping pong, hammocking, and playing the penny whistle. Can you imagine what his neighbors must think?

Yeah. You guessed it: he was homeschooled.

The Traveler's League Book Series was born when he strayed from the normal bedtime routine of reading, and instead created new worlds full of funny characters, action, magic, and adventure. Since then, he has committed himself to entertaining children through writing books that make kids feel the magic of adventure and friendship. All the books in the series are available on Amazon.

Made in the USA
Monee, IL
14 December 2020

52975126R00102